THE FRUITCAKE CHALLENGE

CHALLENGE

By Carrie Fancett Pagels

This book is a work of fiction. Any references to historical events, real people, or real places are used fictitiously. Other names, places, characters, and events are products of the author's imaginations, and any resemblance to actual events or places or persons, living or dead, is entirely coincidental.

First Edition
September 2014
Printed and bound in the United States of America

ISBN-13 978-0-692-29003-3

For contact with the author or speaking engagements, please visit www.CarrieFancettPagels.com

Dedication

To Jeffrey Donald Pagels, my best friend, the love of my life, and the inspiration for so many of my heroes! So glad God blessed me with such a wonderful husband.

And to the memory of my mother, Ruby Evelyn Skidmore Fancett, whose stories of growing up in a lumber camp, assisting her camp cook mother, Eliza Clark Skidmore, inspired this story. My mom really did make "the best fruitcake ever!"

Acknowledgements

First I want to thank God, who has inspired me to write. Couldn't do it without God the Father, Son, and Holy Spirit. Abba Father—every book is for you! I have so many people to thank. I'd like to thank my husband, to whom the story is dedicated, and my son, Clark, for being such a history buff and working on my stories with me. And for his tolerance and accompaniment for all the research trips we did for this novella. He has amazing insight into literary plot devices. Hugs to Cassandra Pagels for bringing DarDar, my big black Labrador retriever grandpuppy, over—he brought back great memories of our family lab, Blue Dog and inspired the addition of Jo's dog in this book! And I'd like to acknowledge Clark's friend, Thomas McWithey, for letting us "borrow" his first name for my hero. A good name.

Thank you to all the wonderful folks at the Tahquamenon Logging Museum, in Newberry, Michigan, in the beautiful Upper Peninsula. I want to acknowledge Rose Anderson, in particular, who has been so supportive of my writing. Thank you to the volunteers and those who've donated to the museum help keep alive the lore of the lumber camps and lumberjacks. The museum has a cook shack and serves lumberjack breakfasts on special occasions, which is a huge labor of love (and which I've greatly enjoyed!) I love this place!

Thank you to the Hartwick Pines staff in Michigan's lower peninsula, which includes one of the last stands of virgin white pine in the state. Walking through this gorgeous protected area of towering trees gives an idea of what it must have been like before these pines were logged out.

Thank you to the staff of White Star ferry lines in St. Ignace, Michigan, in particularly the wonderful young Yoopers at the Railroad ferry dock. Also, I appreciate help I received at the Old Mackinaw Point lighthouse, in Mackinaw City, which is part of the state park system. They have some wonderful pictures and facts about icebreakers that opened up the straits so that railroad cars could be pulled across even in winter.

I'm grateful for Gina Welborn's invitation to contribute to this collection. Participating in the Christmas Traditions authors group has been a great experience. The group includes Cynthia Hickey, the lead, who designed my cover and our banner. Cynthia has also helped those of us who are new to "hybrid" publishing. The members of the Christmas Traditions Promotion Group on Facebook are the best influencers! Big hugs to Linda Marie Finn, Angi Griffis, Diana Montgomery, Sister Mary Lou Kwiatkowski, Nancy McLeroy, Debbie Lynn Costello, Jackie Tessnair, Maxie Lloyd-Hamilton Anderson, Wendy Shoults, Chris Granville, Britney Adams and *Beta readers listed below.

Kudos to *Kathy Maher for help in promoting the novella and for help as critique partner. Big hugs to my professional Beta reader, *Teresa Mathews, for her read through of the manuscript. And more hugs to my other Beta/ARC readers *Anne Payne, *Regina Fujitani, *Bonnie Roof, *Janella Wilson, Melanie Backus, *Tina St. Clair Rice, and *Rosemary "Chicki" Foley (*all of whom are also part of the promo group!) Thank you to Eva Marie Everson for editing. Any errors in the book are my own.

I don't know what I'd do without my blog support system, the ladies are friends as well as amazing bloggers at www.OvercomingWithGod.com blog. Thank you to Diana Flowers, our Senior Reviewer, *Teresa S. Mathews, our poet and reviewer, and to our international reviewer, Noela Nancarrow of Australia. The OWG angels really have blessed me.

Thank you also to the talented bunch of authors at www.ColonialQuills.org. It's been such a blast, and so informative, to hang out with like-minded writers who love colonial and early American history. And our Tea Parties online are the best—even if I say so myself!

Thank you, Dr. Mark Croucher, my chiropractor, for keeping me adjusted so I can write! Hugs to my writing accountability group members: Julie Klassen, Melanie Dickerson and Sarah E. Ladd—you keep my attitude adjusted so I can write and you keep me on track!

Prologue

Near Mackinaw City, Michigan 1890

Vast evergreens crowded the roadway on both sides of the wagon, towering over a hundred feet to the sky, almost obscuring the sunlight. Every time the dray hit a bump in the mucky road, Tom Jeffries grasped his crate of books in one arm and his boxy leather suitcase in the other. After the last spine-jolting rut had been crossed, he pulled out his father's gold pocket watch.

Shouldn't be too much longer now.

He swatted at the mosquitoes that swarmed the deep woods. No wonder the men at the mercantile had laughed when Tom had asked about purchasing arm garters to go with his new work shirts. He'd need to leave his shirt sleeves unrolled, even for summer, to keep the pests off him. Even that wasn't working now, though. Tom draped his Hudson Bay blanket around his shoulders and pulled it up over his neck and then squashed his felt slouch hat down further to cover his forehead.

The vehicle slowed. Sitting in the bed of the flat dray, Tom swiveled so he could see the reason for their halt.

The drayman turned to him, as did his son beside him. "Here's yer camp."

Nothing but woods surrounded them. Tom hesitated. He wasn't about to be dropped off in the middle of nowhere.

The barrel-chested man pointed straight ahead. "That there's Boss Christy's office and the cook shack is beyond."

Tom hopped down, but left his belongings on the wagon bed.

"Ya oughta be glad ya ain't come in with the regular crew, young fella." The driver barked out a laugh. "Ya'd have been trampin' to the camp this ten miles out insteada ridin' plush in the back."

The red-haired youth scowled. "Mister, ain't ya ever been a lumberjack before?"

Ignoring the boy, Tom turned toward the supposed campsite. As he squinted, sunlight pierced the treetops, illuminating a circular clearing of dark earth about fifty feet ahead and a wood-sided hut to the left that blended in with the forest. He stretched out the kinks in his long legs. Thank God the train had gotten him as far north as it had. How had the old timers ever managed riding in a wagon for days?

"Best get your stuff out. I'm gonna turn around down there but it gets tricky with the mud from the rain."

The man's son dropped down and moved to the back of the wagon. "I'll help ya, mister." But when he made to lift Tom's crate of books, the youth stumbled under the weight.

Tom grabbed hold of his treasure trove. "If you could carry that bag," he said, nodding toward the suitcase, "I'd be obliged."

"Yes, sir." Flushed, the boy hoisted down the brown case.

In a short while, Tom's belongings had been deposited on the wood-planked stoop of what passed for an office, and his driver and son had circled the dray around. Other than bird song and wind rustling the tree boughs, there was little sound or movement. Then the wagon's wheels rumbled down the narrow drive, away from the camp.

A now-familiar buzzing tickled Tom's ear. He swatted, then rested his hand along the back and side of his neck. After battling the pests all the way out, welts covered the area. Should have greased himself up with the stinky ointment one of the Chippewa traders in town had offered him. He slapped at another mosquito, pulling his hand away to find blood smeared along the fingertips. He wiped it off on his new dungarees and then knocked on the flimsy pine door.

No answer. He rocked on his feet, a sweet symphony of birdsong echoing all around, as though they'd come out to serenade him on his arrival. Wood smoke wafted from the squat office's chimney. A water pump groaned from behind the building. Tom followed the sound, his new work boots squeaking in protest with each step.

The northwoods were indeed a breath-taking sight, but the young woman standing before him, pumping water, was prettier than any vista he'd ever beheld or any belle he'd ever courted—and there had been many.

Until Papa died, anyways. And until his heart had been broken.

Tom exhaled as loudly as he thought proper, but consumed with pumping water, the girl didn't take note of him. Her bronze hair appeared glazed with copper. The mass flowed down in waves, reminding Tom of the beautiful Tahquamenon Falls—portrayed in painting he'd viewed the previous day. Peaches and cream skin looked the sort to burn if she left her woody bower. And her pink cotton dress strained against decidedly feminine curves with each motion.

"Miss?"

But still, she didn't hear him. Instead, she carried a bucket to a large metal pot hanging over a fire and poured the water in, curls of steam wafting up.

Footfall sounded behind him as the beauty threw a tattered blanket over a line set at eye level. Four ropes had been tied off to poles in a neat smallish square around a tin trough. Suddenly someone clapped a rough hand over Tom's mouth while another burly arm pulled, forcing him to walk backward and around the corner of the building. He stumbled but caught himself. Pain seared his elbow as it rammed into a rock hard gut.

"What are you doin' back here?" The massive hand clasped over Tom's mouth released as the huge man on his left shoved him toward the one on the right.

"You spyin' on our sister?"

"No!" But he had been, of course. Tom swallowed. At 6'3" he wasn't used to being manhandled, nor encountering anyone taller than himself. But the first brother had a good three inches and likely another seventy pounds of solid muscle on him. The giant's upper arm was as big around as Tom's thigh, as was his partner's.

Tom shook his arms hard and the two released him. "No one present at the office when I arrived."

"And who are you?" Despite his whiskers, this man appeared younger, with the unlined face of a youth. With almost-black wavy hair, dark brown eyes, and ruddy complexions beneath their black beards, the two resembled each other. Together, they created a formidable mass of muscle.

"I'm Tom Jeffries, the new man."

The bigger man jerked his thumb toward the front of the building. "That your stuff up there?"

"Yes."

The two exchanged a glance, and then guffawed. "We've got a teacher and an early one for once. And here you look big enough to be our next axman."

Tom averted his gaze. *God, why you are taunting me? I thought you'd guided me here.* "I'm not here for the teaching job."

Educators didn't make enough money to support themselves, much less themselves *and* their mothers. And they must follow a set of rules designed for saints. And from what he'd heard on his trip north, lumberjacks had a code of their own—of the opposite sort. But with Mr. Christy running a "clean family camp" Tom figured he'd be all right. Then again, with these two barbarians, maybe not.

The shorter man extended a hand. "I'm Ox and this is my younger brother, Moose. We're Boss Christy's boys."

Moose's eyes darted back toward where the young woman remained and ignored Tom's offered hand.

Ox slipped his thumbs into his trouser pockets. "Where you think you're gonna keep those books in the bunkhouse?"

How many men slept in the bunkhouse, this being a family camp? "Under my bed."

"You the new axman then?"

"Yes." Tom gritted his teeth.

"Pa's gone to town. Our ma just died and our sister's trying to get ready so we can all go talk with the preacher."

No wonder the men were so irritable. They'd recently lost their mother. "I'm so sorry. Please accept my condolences for your loss."

Moose glared at him. "That's why our sister is back there trying to take a bath."

"Outside?" The word slipped past Tom's lips before he could stop it.

The taller man inclined his head toward Tom. "Mister, there wasn't supposed to be anyone out here."

Ox nodded. "And it's a nice day."

No, it wasn't. It was chilly, maybe in the low 60s.

Tom gestured around the empty circle, edged by equipment, beyond which a string of small cottages or rather shacks extended off into the woods. "Where is everyone?"

"The womenfolk are cooking in their homes and the men have gone ahead out to secure the logging site before we go." Moose scratched at his beard.

"Maybe you can guard while we're gone." Ox pulled on his suspenders. "Most of the folks will go into town."

Moose pressed a broad hand against Ox's plaid chest. "Better guard than you were. You were supposed to make sure no one bothered Jo."

The older brother shoved the younger back. "I had to take care of necessary business."

"Whatever you say, brother." The bigger one rolled his eyes.

His acquiescence surprised Tom. The younger brother seemed like a bully, but when the elder held his ground, the bigger man submitted.

Ox buffed his nails against his wool shirt. "Listen, Jo's our sister and we don't cotton to anyone bothering her, if you take our meaning."

The two men glowered at him with fierce, almost black eyes. Tom didn't need to reweigh in his mind the five hundred or more pounds of solid muscular wall protecting the lovely Jo to steer clear of her—and them.

"I do understand. Perfectly." *What will they do if I stand my ground?* Not that he'd ever want to bother a lady, but what if he wanted to take a stand on anything in this camp, such as courting their sister? He needed this job, didn't need to upset his new boss. No wonder the vast majority of camps didn't allow women.

Mr. Christy sure was taking a chance with his family camp.

Chapter 1

Late August, 1890

Every muscle in Jo Christy's back complained as she repeatedly pressed the Mason jar ring into a continuous sheet of biscuit dough, rolled out atop the oak counter in the lumber camp's kitchen. The only thing that could have made her task more frustrating would be if Tom Jeffries showed up to annoy her with more of his flirtatious questions. In all her twenty-five years, she'd never had a man irritate her the way he did—nor had anyone been so persistent in trying to charm her. Always before, for some reason, they'd given up after only a few attempts.

At the table in the kitchen's center, Mrs. Peyton looked up from her task of mixing more dough. Only a few of her gray curls peeked out from beneath her head wrap. Jo had a devil of a time trying to keep her thick mane of hair covered and secured, especially without Ma there to help her.

At the end of the long rectangular wood structure that formed the cookhouse, the door swung open, admitting additional light onto the far end of the pine floors. From his bed in the corner, Blue Dog raised his hundred pounds of blue-black Labrador flesh and issued a low growl as a man entered the room. Jo wiped the back of her hand over her brow.

Nearby, her youngest cooking assistant at eighteen, Ruth, rested her hand on an aged cleaver in the block while Mrs. Peyton pulled her heavy wood rolling pin into her hand. The hair on the back of Jo's neck bristled. Blue growled at only one man—Tom. And the occasional peddler who had the poor sense to come to the cook shack first and not the office.

"Good afternoon, ladies!" Pa's best axman swaggered toward the counter. Blue followed him, still growling, his teeth bared.

The lumberjack ignored him.

How in one short month had Jo's life been turned upside down? The same week her mother had died, she'd taken on Ma's job as head cook. That was when this know-it-all Tom Jeffries had shown up in their camp.

Tom removed his knit Frenchmen's hat and wadded it in his right hand. "May I say—you ladies all are quite a lovely sight for a man to behold in these north woods."

Jo squeezed her eyes closed. Still angry with God over Ma's death, she didn't pray to the Lord about this situation so much as she willed herself to not explode at Tom. She prided herself on being even-tempered. Not so with this arrogant axman.

When Jo opened her eyes, Mrs. Peyton faced her, her knowing expression urging Jo to let her handle the latest question from Tom—one that surely would be posed once he reached them.

Jo turned away as his boots clunked closer. She inhaled deeply and went to the far wall where they'd been slicing strawberries for the evening meal—a real treat and the last of the summer fruit. She sifted sugar over each bowl, stirred, and then waited.

"How can we help you, Mr. Jeffries?" Mrs. Peyton asked.

"Ma'am, for starters you can call me Tom." Even with her back turned, Jo could hear the man rocking back and forth in his hard-soled boots.

Mrs. Peyton sighed. "Did you have a question about dinner tonight?"

"Again?" Ruth added, her tone sweet, and her voice soft. But Jo knew what she thought of Tom's presence.

"No, ma'am. I heard we're having roast pork and potatoes. And I can smell those fresh strawberries and your sisters, Ruth, are bringing up the cream to be whipped soon. I helped them some, too." From his tone, Jo surmised he was wheedling a compliment from their senior cook.

Instead, silence hung in the dough-scented air.

"What do you want then, Mr. Jeffries?" Ruth's voice held an edge sharper than the knife Jo just lifted from the counter—one her brothers had scraped on the stone the night before. The blade glinted in the sunlight.

"I had a question about Miss Christy."

Jo stiffened, almost dropping the sharp implement in her hand.

"I just keep wondering…"

The door slammed shut as someone else entered. Blue Dog's nails clicked over the pine planks. Split firewood rattled and banged against each other as it was dropped into the box. Must be her friend, Sven. Jo's brothers hadn't even brought kindling in for their afternoon cooking or for the evening meal.

"What were you wondering, Mr. Jeffries?" Ruth's voice had turned sweet as the maple syrup that had topped the men's flapjacks that morning. Yup, that had to be Sven who'd walked in.

Jo turned and looked directly into the piercing eyes of the too-handsome axman.

Now her mouth went dry as she faced their newest lumberjack. "Too pretty for his own good" Pa had said about him. With light brown hair and changeable green and gold eyes, Tom's presence was palpable.

"Why is a lovely gal like you still unmarried?" Although he didn't say it, she heard the unspoken "at your age." Under his left arm, he clutched a thick book against his side. Right now, Jo wanted to grab it and whack his head with it.

Every day, Jo wondered the same thing Tom had asked. Why *hadn't* she found a mate?

Anger popped through her like a pine branch thrown in a fire. Blue Dog trotted up to the counter, Sven right behind him.

"Jeffries?" Sven's blue eyes lit briefly on Ruth before he fixed his attention on Tom. As their longest serving lumberjack—despite being one of the youngest—Sven often assumed the "take charge" attitude Jo heard in his voice. "Are you daft, man? Didn't Ox and Moose tell you to stay out of here? They told you to stay away from Jo, just like they've told every other man who has come through this camp."

Jo cringed. Was that true?

Tom swiveled toward Sven. Although Tom stood a couple of inches taller, Sven possessed a good stone's weight muscle more than Tom. But Sven was gentle as a kitten. At least with Jo. And, the Good Lord knew, especially with Ruth and her sisters.

Sighing, she hung her head. She'd heard her brothers had kept the men away from her but she hadn't been sure. Until now. Sven would never lie about that. And if her brothers told Tom to stay away, they must have thought the new lumberjack had some kind of

13

interest in her—other than having his belly filled. A sick feeling started in her gut.

Sven bent over and rubbed Blue's head. "What a good boy you are."

"Doesn't like me," Tom mumbled.

Jo snickered. "Shows he's a smart dog, too."

Tom's gold-flecked green eyes pierced hers and she immediately regretted her words.

Beside her, Mrs. Peyton and Ruth chuckled.

The door flew open again and Ox and Moose lumbered toward them. The room measured over sixty feet long, but her brothers crossed it in a flash. Jo threw up her hands to halt Ox's final charge but he and Moose strode forward, their heavy footfalls causing the unlit kerosene lanterns overhead to swing, until they came alongside Tom.

"You bothering our sister again?" Ox slammed one of his meaty fists into his open palm.

"Yes, I am. And I intend to persist in speaking the truth about her many lovely attributes." Tom cocked his head to the side and grinned at Moose, as though he was a woodpecker about to get himself some bugs.

Mrs. Peyton brought a wooden spoon down on the serving counter. "Now listen here. Pestering a gal with questions and then telling her she's an old maid hardly count as good courting behavior. You young folks need to take a lesson or two from your elders."

Color washed Tom's high cheekbones. "Yes, ma'am, but haven't I told Miss Christy every day how pretty she is? How her hair is lovelier than the oak leaves?"

Protest she might, but all those little compliments of his had, truthfully, lifted her spirits during these past dark weeks. Ordinarily the vibrant autumn colors cheered her. But not this season. Not without Ma.

Thinking back over Tom's many comments she realized something. Until today her brothers had been nowhere nearby to hear Tom's frequent flattery.

"Miss Christy, I believe I have your problem figured out."

"My problem?"

"I know precisely why you're in your predicament and they are standing right behind me."

Jo felt her eyes widen at his bravado. No one ever stood up to her brothers.

Ox shoved Tom's shoulder. "What's that?"

Tom pushed her brother's hand away and leaned in closer to him, pointing his finger in Ox's face, like a teacher scolding a pupil. "Your sister is slaving away back here, unmarried, because you two threaten to pummel anyone who comes near her."

He rocked back on his heels as her brothers exchanged glances.

"So?" Ox didn't sound the least bit concerned.

Tom frowned. "Doesn't it bother you that she could be happier if she were allowed to be courted?"

The scent of sugar, strawberries, and dough accompanied the two other cooks as on either side they pressed closer to Jo. Each placed a hand on Jo's back, like two guardian angels protecting her. Across the counter, Sven stared at the plank floor.

Moose squared his shoulders. "Pa did let her be courted—he told Sven here he could spend time with Jo."

Grinning, Ox slapped Sven's back. "Heck, we've all known Sven since he was fifteen. He's like another brother."

Sven's cheeks grew red as his chest pushed out from Ox's wallop. "*Tack.* Thank you. Yes, many years ago Mr. Christy bestowed his *förtroende*, his trust in me."

Jo's jaw flexed. Pa had given his trust to Sven, yes, but only as her friend. Lately, Pa was too grief-stricken to even respond to card-playing requests from his closest friends.

Ruth gave Jo's back a gentle pat; unlike the whack Ox had given Sven, then turned and took Jo's former place by the strawberries. *Clunk, clunk, clunk*; she sliced her knife through the fruit onto the wood board with a vengeance.

Sven frowned at Moose and Ox.

"And you two still haven't tied the knot." Tom's voice held a question.

Jo felt like grabbing the rolling pin from Mrs. Peyton and clobbering her brothers with it. "Gentlemen, I have dinner to get ready. Sven, you're welcome to stay—the rest of you be gone or we won't feed you tonight and I mean it."

Tom stared slack-jawed at Sven then returned his gaze to Jo. "Miss Christy, I apologize for my egregious behavior. Please forgive me."

Egregious? What did that mean? Sounded like a disease. She gave a curt nod to dismiss him, and Tom and her brothers departed.

And not a moment too soon.

What on earth had gotten into him since entering this logging camp? Tom ran a hand back through his thick hair and perched, slumped over, on the end of his wood-framed bunk bed. Maybe it was the long hours of physical labor or the lack of sleep. He needed to make himself a new bunk, like the big Christy brothers had done, adding extra length so he didn't have to sleep with his feet hanging off the end of the thin mattress. He'd shared a room once before, at Ohio Normal School for Teachers, but that was much different than sharing a huge bunkhouse with fifty snoring shanty boys. The stench proclaimed the number of those who failed to groom themselves properly. Regardless of his own efforts to keep himself presentable, he'd had no luck getting Miss Christy's attention. And after tonight, he likely never would.

Who'd have thought that Jo Christy had her cap set for quiet Sven? And what had prevented them from marrying? It all seemed so clear to him now that her brothers had told him. Jo and Sven walking together. Jo and Sven watching Ruth's young sisters when the girl needed privacy. When she wasn't helping in the kitchen, the eighteen-year-old blonde watched over her siblings while her father worked in the camp. Often, even after work, Ruth's widowed father would run off and play cards and visit at other cabins. Mr. Christy frowned upon gambling and ran a clean camp, but the boss mourned his wife too much to notice the problems.

Heavy footfall lumbered toward him.

"What you got there?" Moose grabbed Tom's copy of *Adventures of Tom Sawyer* but he held fast and pulled it back.

"A good book by Mark Twain."

"Can I borrow it sometime?" The big man ran his hand across his square jaw.

"Sure." Tom handed the novel to him.

"Thanks." He opened the cover, his mouth slackening in surprise. "This is signed."

Tom's face heated. He resisted the urge to grab the tome back. Twain had signed the copy and presented it to Tom's father, a professor, when the author had visited Western Reserve College for a lecture.

He shrugged. "It was a gift." His statement was true; the volume had been a gift—to his father.

"Oh." Moose cocked his head. "The men have a betting pool going on. We're wagerin' on how much schoolin' you have, Tom."

He laughed. "They'll bet on anything, won't they?"

"It's up to ten dollars now."

Tom whistled. No wonder Ox had been peppering him with questions recently, about what he did before working in the woods. He'd told Jo's brother that if his father needed that information he'd be happy to share it. That quieted him for a while.

"Hoping to bring some of my collection to the school house." Tom ran a hand over the rough wool blanket that covered his bed, then bent and tapped the wooden side of his crate of books.

"Where'd you get all those?"

"Here and there." What did it matter?

Moose arched a black eyebrow at him. "The kids might enjoy nighttime stories after dinner, if you're of a mind to read to them."

Anticipation shot through Tom, and he worked to squelch the sensation. He was a lumberjack now. But he'd seen how the kids, with the days being so long during the summer, were sometimes at a loss for what to do. "Would your father mind?"

"Nah. He loves to read. Used to read to the kids himself before Ma got sick."

For some reason that image touched Tom. He could picture the burly man, with his animated features, offering a compelling read to the tykes.

Would Jo approve? He rubbed his chin. Not that it mattered. The lovely young woman was taken. Still, the idea of such a strong-willed beauty paired with the quiet Sven didn't match up. Such relationships sometimes worked out, if that was what each preferred. But why then, did he think she might care for him? Maybe because her fair skin often blushed a pretty pink, beneath her auburn curls, when he came near her.

Moose snapped his suspenders. "As you know, all of us lumberjacks can tell a tall tale—but I feel pretty certain the kids have heard them all by now. We've been in this camp three years now. Probably have to pull up stakes sometime in the next year or so."

"I don't mind. I'll do it." Tom pulled the wooden box further out from beneath the bed, and selected a story for that night. "For the kids." Maybe Jo would come and listen, too.

A grin split Moose's ruddy face. "I'll go tell Ruth. She'll let the others know."

Ox and Sven entered through a nearby door.

Sven headed to his bunk and Jo's younger brother joined them. "What are you two cookin' up?"

Moose jerked a thumb toward Tom. "He's gonna read to the kids like Pa used to do."

To Tom's surprise, Ox smiled and smacked Tom on the shoulder. "That'll make Ruth happy."

Moose nodded. "Yeah, she's always looking for a way to keep her sisters out of trouble at night."

Ox tapped the front of Moose's red and black checked shirt. "We'll announce it at dinner tonight."

Tom's stomach growled. "Think Jo will let us eat?"

"Yeah. She will."

Moose frowned. "Someone has to go round to the cabins and let the families know, too. And I was just gonna take a lie down, like Sven."

From the other end of the room, snoring announced that the lumberjack was fast asleep.

Ox yawned. "Me, too."

"I'll make rounds." Tom couldn't sleep in the afternoon, like some of the men did. If he napped, he'd be awake all night listening to the cacophony of noises in the room. Besides which, thoughts of a certain auburn-haired beauty already kept him awake.

Chapter 2

Late September

Jo lowered herself to the rough plank bench behind the cook shack, bent over, and cupped her hands in the fresh spring water. She drew it up and splashed her face over and over again. If only doing so would help her recall her purpose—that she had to tell Pa she needed out of the camp and into the real world beyond the forest.

Although her lashes, beaded with water, obscured her view, she heard Tom's jaunty whistling before he rounded the corner. She closed her eyes and hurriedly blotted her face with a clean kitchen towel.

"Miss Christy?"

"Yes, Mr. Jeffries?"

"I have a conundrum."

"What?" She didn't need to hear about his personal problems or whatever that was. Probably another disease like egreeg-something-or-other was.

He pulled off his Frenchman's cap. "You see, I visited the cottages…"

It pleased her that he didn't call them shacks the way everyone else did. Like she, herself, did.

"And, at every stop the lady of the house extolled your virtues and gifted me with so many items for you that I am uncertain where to put them."

Jo blinked up at the man. Sven rounded the corner, pulling a child's wagon piled with an assortment of goods, ranging from what looked like a pair of knit slippers to a crate marked "Apples."

"Everyone said they miss seeing you."

Since Ma died and Jo had assumed her position, she hadn't had the energy at night necessary to visit around the camp as she had when she was just a kitchen assistant. Instead, she now fell asleep almost as soon as her head settled on her feather pillow.

Tom gestured toward the cart. "They wanted to thank you for all the help you used to give them—before your mother passed."

"I …" Unbidden tears overflowed and she dabbed at her cheeks. "Thank you."

Sven pulled the wagon toward the kitchen storage shack. "Why don't I put this in here until after dinner, Jo?"

She sniffed. "Yes, but bring the crate of apples in for tonight, please—the men will like the extra fruit."

Tom saluted her. "Yes, ma'am." He grabbed the box and hoisted it onto his shoulder as though it weighed nothing. "And may I say the ladies have sung your praises far more prettily than I ever could."

Not sure what to say, she simply stared at his broad back as he departed. Then curiosity got the better of her and she went to the kitchen shack and began to pull items from the wagon. The small gloves would be perfect for Ruth, as were the slippers. Mrs. Peyton could use the blue wool scarf. So many lovely gifts, all which could be shared.

After dinner had been served, Jo and her crew quickly divided the contents in the wagon. The women hugged and thanked her for their goodies. After they'd gone, all Jo wanted to do was rinse off in the river and go to bed. But she dare not go down alone, so she walked around to the front of the cook shack to listen to Tom read.

Frogs' ribbits competed with the noise of the fire crackling in the clearing. Children ringed the circle, most nestled on their mother's or father's laps. Seated on a stump, Tom Jeffries raised his index finger to his mouth, licked it, and then used his damp fingertip to turn the page of his book.

Jo crossed her arms and listened from the stoop. Tom's deep melodic voice carried across the hard-packed dirt yard where the humusy smell of earth competed with wood and tobacco smoke.

He was reading one of her favorites—*Pinocchio.*

There was a good moral lesson in that story. Lies always resulted in problems. She frowned. Was it a lie to let Tom believe that Sven still courted her or had any interest in her other than as friend? They had come to the conclusion years earlier that they were suited only as companions. Besides, she'd seen how Ruth looked at him, and Sven at her.

Pinocchio was a puppet. Well, sometimes she felt like one too—at Ma's bidding for so many years, helping her in the kitchen.

And now at Pa's, at least until he found someone to take over the kitchen. But being there made her feel close to Ma. Her eyes filled with tears. This Christmas Ma had promised she could talk with Pa about leaving the camp. Ma had said she would support her. Now, instead, Christmas would be another chore and a reminder that Ma had died.

Jo sat on the split log bench beside the lunch hall and rested her back against the unpainted wood building. Sunlight faded above the hundred-foot treetops.

Her eyelids grew heavy. And before she knew it, she had fallen asleep.

A gentle shake of her shoulder woke her. The touch was too gentle to be her brother's, but firmer than Sven's. She looked up into a handsome shadowed face, not sure if she was dreaming.

Tom Jeffries bent over her, bringing with him the pleasant scent of hair pomade. He rested a book against his thigh.

"Miss Christy, it isn't safe to be sleeping out here on the bench."

She frowned. "Of course not." Where were her brothers?

"Everyone's gone to their cabins, miss."

She and Tom were out here alone? *Not possible.*

"Sven?" She scanned the rapidly darkening yard. Ghostly lamplight bobbed along in the direction of the cabins.

"I asked him to walk Ruth and her sisters home. Gave him my lantern to use."

A full moon hung overhead, gently illuminating the yard but as one moved back into the woods it would be too dark to see without a kerosene lamp.

"Oh." She ran her tongue over her dry lips.

"Your brothers are still down playing cards with the Everetts."

They'd left her. A swirl of emotions began in her belly— outrage that they'd forgotten to walk her home, gratitude toward Tom, resentment at his constant badgering of her, and shock that he'd dismissed her friend Sven. And somehow, freedom to make her own choices blew away the other concerns like a Mackinaw gale.

"Let me escort you home, Miss Christy. I believe your father took to his bed early tonight."

"Yes, thank you." What was happening here? She sounded like her true self, not the shrew she'd turned into whenever Tom came around.

Jo rose and he offered her support. She slid her hand into the crook of his elbow and he pulled her close to his side, the warmth of his body sending shivers through her. She slowed her steps and pulled free, clasping her arms across her abdomen. The evening chill made her tremble. Tom removed his wool jacket and settled it around her shoulders. To her surprise, the soft coat brought her a sense of comfort. She looked up at him. No one, other than Pa, had ever offered his garment to her.

"Sorry I sent your beau on his way, Miss Christy. But Ruth's sisters were running in all directions and Sven seemed to know just what to say to get them to mind."

Jo laughed. "I think they're afraid of him, even though he'd never harm a fly."

"Hmmm, I think if something riled him up you'd see some action out of Sven."

In the twilight she observed him chewing his lower lip. Something within, the nudging of her conscience perhaps, loosened her lips. "Sven and I have known each other for years. We've been great *friends*." There. That should help Tom understand. But why did she need him to know?

She was so tired, she wasn't thinking straight.

"Oh!" Stumbling, she almost sank to her knees, but Tom caught her beneath her arm and pulled her up.

"Are you all right?"

What a question. Her mother had died, her brothers had chased away any possible beaus, Sven had gone off with Ruth, and her father seemed lost in his own grief.

"I'm fine."

"Good." There was a softness in his voice she hadn't heard before.

They walked in silence beneath the full moon until they reached what was the closest thing to a "home" as she'd ever had and stopped in front of the shack she shared with her Pa.

"Here you are, miss."

Had the checkered curtains parted by Pa's bed or was it her imagination?

Tom lifted her fingertips upward, toward his lips.

He was going to kiss her hand! And she'd not yet rubbed lanolin into her rough skin. She pulled away. Her cheeks heated. After all, why should she care if he kissed her chafed hand?

"My apologies, Miss Christy. And good evening."

Tom held his tongue for three long weeks after the embarrassing episode when Jo had yanked her hand from his, like he was some gypsy peddler come to carry her off. Every day he tramped to the logging site and then back the miles to the camp. Today, after seeing Sven and Ruth together, he couldn't resist a jibe. He swaggered toward the lunch counter, behind which Mrs. Peyton and Jo were peeling potatoes and laughing.

"Where's your little helper?" Tom grabbed an apple from a big bowl on the nearest table.

Jo and Mrs. Peyton exchanged a sideways glance.

The auburn-haired beauty arched a brow. "If you mean Ruth, her sisters are home from school, ill."

"They're no more ill than you or me, Miss Christy." Tom bit into the apple.

Her glare was no worse than the shanty boys were when he stopped spinning a yarn halfway through and made them wait for the rest of a story. "Sven will tell you the same."

"I just came from their house. Sven was out back playing catch with them."

Jo wiped her hands on her red and white checked apron as she stood. She sure was pretty, with tendrils of hair wisping around her face. She drew closer and his cheeks warmed under her scrutiny. "Mr. Jeffries, what business is it of yours what Ruth's sisters do?"

"I just thought you might want to know that your beau is spending time with your helper. Just trying to help is all."

Jo's rosy lips parted, the full lower lip hanging open. Her hazel eyes scanned his face as her brow furrowed. "I think it might be more worthy of your time to find out why the girls are not wanting to go to school."

When his own mouth gaped open, he knew she had him. He'd come in here hoping to stir up a reaction out of Jo, to see if her tale about only being friends with Sven was true. He pressed his lips closed, turned on his heel, and left. Behind him the ladies cackled like the hens out back clucked whenever Tom came near. They didn't like him either. But, today he scored a victory when Blue Dog followed him out of the cookhouse as Jo hollered for her pet to come back.

Chapter 3

Aching everywhere, Jo's body screamed that she was too young to feel this old. She settled gingerly onto her work chair in the kitchen. Even Ruth looked peaked sitting slumped over a bowl of potatoes, peeling slower than Jo had ever observed her doing. Yesterday, Jo and her assistants had prepared a late October Harvest festival feast—enough to feed the fifty single men and all the families, too. They'd had little extra help, save from the wives who'd offered their assistance to the kitchen crew.

The door opened then slammed behind "Mr. Cocky" himself, as the lead axman, Tom Jeffries, entered the cookhouse.

"Here comes trouble," Jo murmured.

She and her kitchen crew ceased cutting biscuits on the flour-dusted table. Although she already knew Tom had no business in her domain at this time, a glance at the clock confirmed his too-early arrival for dinner yet again. The hall was empty save for her and the other cooks, which was just the way she liked it. Soon enough every table would be filled with rowdy lumberjacks who'd inhale their food in minutes, and probably without so much as a "thank you" or "that was good." Never mind that she and the other ladies had labored almost all day to prepare their meal.

At least Tom was polite and he had complimented them often on their cooking skills—she'd give the handsome devil that.

As he neared the table, her annoyance and her heart rate increased. Why was he always so smooth? Why did Tom Jeffries, with his gentlemanly manners, rub her as raw as a pair of new shoes? He tucked his thumbs inside the waistband of his dun-colored work pants and squared his broad shoulders.

"Good day ladies. I thought I'd let you know about my special announcement."

Jo eyed the wooden spatula directly on the counter in front of the man. Although he stood a head taller than she was, she'd like nothing more than to pop him good on the forehead and see if that put some sense in him.

Mrs. Peyton stood and sighed. "Whatchya got to share, Thomas?"

His syrupy smile made Jo want to roll her eyes. But the single dimple in his cheek begged her fingertips to smooth a wayward lock of maple-colored hair away from it. He stretched his arms wide. The man just wanted to show off his big shoulders and broad chest, which had filled out even more in the months since he'd arrived. This man was stirring up feelings in her that Jo didn't need. She'd give him till the count of ten and then she'd throw him out of her kitchen.

Tom puffed out his chest like a banty rooster. "I have decided that I'll marry any gal…"

His luminous eyes met hers. "…who can bake a fruitcake just like my mother makes every Christmas."

"Dontcha say?" Jo's relief assistant, Irma—a woman who looked a decade older than her seventy years—laughed.

Jo choked on her own spit. Ruth patted her back.

Tom tugged at his shirt collar. He unbuttoned the top button, freeing his bulky neck and a tuft of golden-brown hair. "It'll be Christmas before you know it and I'm yearning for fruitcake. I figured this would be a way to quell that urge."

Quell his urge indeed. The only thing she'd quell was the headache he was giving her—and she'd do that by grabbing her broom and chasing him outside. Quell his urge—who spoke like that anyway? No lumberjack she knew.

She stared at him for a moment, flummoxed—a big word she knew well, for Tom caused her to feel that way much of the time.

Tom's full lips bunched, then twitched. "I mean it, Miss Christy. I keep my word." He placed a wide hand over his heart.

Apparently she was supposed to have jumped at his offer. *Of all the nerve.*

A plan began to bubble up inside her, chasing off her anger and making her want to laugh. All she had to do to bring the cocky axman down a notch or three was to meet his challenge and then refuse his proposal. Yes, that was exactly what she would do! Why, with her baking skills there was no doubt she could prepare a mouth-watering fruitcake that would put his mother's to shame. After all, hadn't she won every blue ribbon in the county for baking since they'd set up this frozen God-forsaken logging camp three years earlier? Before that, Mama had set records back home in Kentucky for her cooking—God rest her soul. Moisture pricked Jo's eyes. If only Ma was here now to help her put this man in his place.

Tom stepped closer, his toffee-colored eyebrows joining together beneath the wavy bangs on his forehead. Behind Jo, Mrs. Peyton cleared her throat as she returned to rolling her biscuits. Jo turned around and caught the wink she gave her. The middle-aged woman rubbed her hands together and stepped toward the counter.

"Now, Tom, see here—I think yer gonna be creatin' a dad-burned problem in the camp."

Jo grabbed potholders and then lifted the two trays of steaming cornbread and set them on a rack to cool. She turned around to face Tom, again. He'd stepped closer, and one side of his mouth twitched as though he was stifling a laugh.

"How do you mean, Mrs. Peyton?" He smiled at the woman. "And may I say, you look fetching today in that blue dress?"

"Pshaw, I'm not havin' none of your sweet talk, Mr. Jeffries. You see here!" She shook a pudgy finger at him. "Why once all the ladies hear about your offer, they'll be trying to cook up a fruitcake for you and then they'd divorce their husbands when they win."

Tom's lips formed an "O." "Hadn't figured on that, Mrs. Peyton."

"Might give you pause to consider your offer." The cook tapped a moccasined foot. "Why, what would my husband say?"

Jo chuckled. She grabbed a sugar cookie left over from the night before and tossed it to Tom before she could even stop herself. Why was she giving a treat to this infuriating man? He nabbed the cookie without hesitation. Blue Dog rose from his bed in the far corner and ambled toward them.

"Good catch." She wasn't reluctant to bestow praise when it was due.

The thing was—Tom Jeffries never received a good word from her lips. Which was wrong. Jo knew her Bible and her Lord well enough to know what God thought about such behavior. Surely it wouldn't be wrong, in fact it would be the correct way to act, to be more polite and attentive to him—just like she was with all the men in the camp. Except they didn't all aggravate the tarnation out of her. Still, the good Word said she should be kind and considerate. Which meant she could toss him an occasional compliment without it meaning she was chasing him.

Tom gave her a slow grin. "Um-hmm," he replied around a mouthful of the sweet cookie, her specialty.

Shanty boys, after eating her rich fudge sauce and whipped vanilla crème on top of one of her huge sugar cookies, claimed they'd died and gone to heaven.

Blue stopped beside Tom. When the man made a slicing motion with his hand, her dog sat. Then to her astonishment, Tom broke his treat into quarters and offered one to her pet, who gulped it down and panted for more, his long black tail thumping the floor.

The little traitor.

Tom made a smoother motion with his outstretched arm.

"Down," he instructed Blue and her dog sank to the floor, his big pink tongue hanging out as Tom bent and gave him another piece of cookie. "Good boy."

He was spoiling her companion and stealing his affections.

"I finally got Garrett and Richard trained to not give Blue food from their plates and then you come along." Jo stomped her boot on the wood floor, causing a bowl on the table to wobble. She grabbed it.

Tom straightened and quirked an eyebrow at her.

Warmth like melting butter slid from the top of her head all the way to her toes. Even her body was betraying her now. She rubbed one foot against another. Maybe soon Pa would give her enough money to purchase a new dress and boots. With winter coming on she'd soon need to wear something extra, even in the kitchen—the floor boards often allowed frigid air to gust up once snow started. Even gussied up, she'd probably not look as pretty as all the gals Tom used to call on in Ohio. And she sure wasn't as educated.

Jo exhaled more loudly than she intended. Tom might be the handsomest, smartest, and strongest axman Pa had ever had in his camp, but he also had arrogance enough for three lumberjacks, all strapped together high atop a log pile about to be floated down river. This latest stunt of proposing such a challenge irked her. And getting her dog to obey him? She was gonna fix him but good.

Blue Dog remained glued to Tom's side. "Who are Garrett and Richard?"

"My brothers." They weren't going to like Tom knowing that information.

"I see." A smile tugged at the corner of his mouth.

She needed to get him out of her kitchen before that cute grin of his made her knees wobble again.

"Well, Tom, I'm real glad you're enjoying my sugar cookies but we've got work to do before dinner is served. Anything else we can do for you?" She affected a soft Kentucky accent like her mother's and met his gaze dead on. She didn't flinch—not even when his eyes softened.

Tom averted his gaze from the lovely cook, considering. Jo Christy still couldn't stand him. No doubt about it. So why did he delight in tormenting her? Maybe the accounting he'd done that morning had freed his tongue. Since his time in the camp, he'd made enough money to send some home plus keep plenty back for his own savings. His mother's letters recently took a turn and she'd expressed a cockamamie idea of starting a business. If Father weren't already dead, the notion would have put him in the grave. Times were changing. His broken engagement to Dr. Eugenia Musgrove was proof of that. The love of his life had found a better offer than a poor schoolteacher could provide—one that included a husband and a medical practice in New York.

Two long years had passed and his heart had finally begun to mend.

"I'll bid my *adieu*." He nodded at Jo and she turned away to her cook stove.

He'd give Jo Christy one thing—she was the first woman he'd met who'd not batted her eyelashes at him and encouraged his attentions. Of course she was the first young lady he'd met since becoming a lumberjack. Before his father had died, the girls back in Ohio flirted, coming up with one excuse after the other to have their fathers drive them by his family's farm. Of course that was before the years with Eugenia, while he waited for her to finish her medical training.

He gritted his teeth and rubbed his jaw.

Tom closed the cookhouse door behind him, and then trotted across the yard. The muck portended a moderate Christmas ahead. He frowned as he entered the bunkhouse, anticipating the stench of single men who didn't see the need of regular bathing. Being a family camp meant there were a large number of families with a lumberjack father. Those people lived in cabins clustered near the cookhouse. And Tom was fairly sure those cottages smelled as good as Jo Christy's kitchen did.

From across the long rectangular building, the bulky Christy brothers looked up from where they bent over a pine log framed bunk.

"What are you working on, Garrett and Richard?" Which one was which?

Ox shoved a broad hand through his thick black hair. "Reckon this is a long enough bunk for you, *Thomas*?"

Only his mother called him Thomas, and then only when angry with him. He stiffened. "Don't call me Thomas."

The man popped his giant fist into his hand. "Then don't call me Garrett—it's Ox."

The taller brother stood from the end of the bed, a hammer in his hand. "And I'd best not hear you calling me *Richard*. Call me Moose, like I told you. Especially if you want me to finish up this extra-long bunk. Then your big old feet will fit in your bed—like mine do now."

"All right, Ox." Then to the other. "Moose."

The younger brother gestured overhead with his tool. "Won't put no jack hanging overhead, either."

With his new lengthier bed at the end of the row, Tom might even be able to pull it nearer the wall to get a little more privacy. To what did he owe this favor by the Christy men?

"Thank you, gentlemen." Tom grinned, but the brothers only grunted. "I'm obliged to you."

"You speak like you got yourself a teacher's education." Ox's dark eyes narrowed. "I've bet fifteen dollars you went to one of them special schools."

"Maybe I did." The Ohio Normal School, where he'd shared a room for the first time in his life.

Moose wiped his forehead with a meaty hand. "Our sister won't be marrying any shanty boy."

"Nope." Ox agreed.

"And why is that?"

With her father and brothers lumberjacks, why wouldn't she?

The brothers exchanged a glance and then attempted to stare him down. "If you were an educated man. A teacher, though—we might let you court her."

What about their father? Mr. Christy's deep sorrow seemed to make the boss's step drag slower each day. He didn't want to upset the man, but from everything he'd heard, he was a feisty and jolly fellow before he lost his wife. And he wanted nothing but his daughter's happiness—and so did Tom.

He cocked his hip and pulled off his gloves, then removed his jacket and hung it and his hat on nearby pegs in the wall. "I've already declared a fruitcake wager, gentlemen. A challenge to your sister."

"What?" Moose swung the hammer one last time, attaching the bunk legs to the frame.

Tom flinched from the loud reverberation in the bunkhouse.

Ox yanked on the leg, which held firm to the frame, but pulled the bunk from the wall. "Pa frowns on gambling—as long as he doesn't catch us at poker."

"You know, gents, we have lumberjack games all the time. Did it ever occur to you that your sister might enjoy a sporting event?"

Again the Christy brothers exchanged a glance, but this time they moved closer. "Jo ain't one for games."

Ox gripped Tom's collar but he didn't flinch, not even as the unmistakable odor of chewing tobacco threatened to overpower him. "Are ... you ... an ... educated ... man?"

Moose squeezed Tom's upper arm. "You've got the arms of a lumberjack now but if you want to avoid a thrashing you better answer Ox's question."

They meant it.

"Yes. I am." Would their father have him thrown out of the camp? Or did they believe he was toying with their sister's affections?

The brothers exchanged a long glance. And then Moose released him.

"We have a proposition for you, then."

Outside, behind the cook shack, Jo plunked herself down on the wooden bench, in the frail November sunshine, and splayed her legs in front of her. One toe tried to push through the torn stitching in her worn leather work boots. She heard the door swing open behind her. The newest cook, Pearl—a handsome woman in her sixties—handed Jo a white and multi-colored striped Hudson Bay blanket. With Pearl on board, Jo finally got some relief in her work.

"Here. Cover up, girlie." Pearl bent and arranged the soft cover around Jo's legs.

Unbidden tears pricked Jo's eyes. "Thank you."

"Ain't nothin' anybody with eyes wouldn't have brought out to you. Problem is you got a hen house full of gals all stirred up over that big galoot, Tom."

Vigorous scratching sounded on the door. *Blue Dog.* Pearl let him out.

"Miss Josephine, if you don't think everybody notices how distracted you are when Tom is around then you aren't using those pretty eyes of yours."

Blue whined and flopped down on her feet. "Poor dog has had to eat my burned biscuits two nights in a row."

"And I'm new out here, but I reckon your Pa wouldn't be allowing those Avery brothers nor about another half dozen of those single men to be chattin' you up and eyein' you if he weren't mournin' your Ma. Am I right?"

Jo shivered as a gust of icy air blew toward them, stirring piles of leaves beneath the tall oaks. "My brothers normally put a stop to any of that nonsense, but lately…"

"The way I see it, miss—and mind you, I've only been here a few days—is that if you make this here Tom believe you really want to win his contest, then maybe some of those other fellas will back off."

"Pearl, if I don't win his challenge all those lumberjacks will laugh me out of this camp—I guarantee it. I will be humiliated."

"They sure do like their jokes." Pearl blew out a puff of breath.

"I'm gonna get him good. You just watch and see."

"I believe ya girlie—and all of us are gonna help you."

Chapter 4

Mid-November

Sven swiped three fruitcake muffins from the tray with one pass. Jo smiled as Ruth wagged her finger at him. "How are we going to make him pay for those, Jo?"

"Refill the kerosene lamps before you leave, Sven. We'll need to light them all soon." Why hadn't Tom snuck in before dinner, like Sven had, to talk with them?

"The days sure are getting short." Sven walked through the kitchen, Blue Dog trailing him, sniffing his pocket for treats. But he came up empty unlike with Tom's, which always held a biscuit or two for her pet.

Kerosene and the like were kept in a shed separate from the tinned goods they kept in the other building.

When Pa went into town, Jo was going to go with him to make sure she had everything for the Thanksgiving feast and to see what dried fruit they had in stock. Just making this recipe of Ruth's had exhausted all their supply of raisins and thankfully all of the rye flour she'd wanted to use up. And making this hearty fruitcake was one way to accomplish her aim. Plus she was pretty sure from what her brothers told her that Tom was from an English background and would prefer a sweeter and lighter recipe in keeping with English tradition.

Ruth took a small bite of one of the muffins. "Jo, I think my mother's recipe tastes wonderful."

The Swedish recipe wasn't one Jo liked, with its dense texture. She laughed. "So did Sven."

The golden-haired man returned and set about refilling the lanterns.

Pearl and Ruth began wrapping the muffins to be packed into the men's lunches for the following day. Good thing those men made coffee all day at the camp because by this time tomorrow the cake would be like hardtack, and would need to be doused in the steaming brew. She'd have to tell Pa. But she'd still been harboring some anger toward him that she'd have to let go. Part of her wanted him to bite into the hard bread and get an unpleasant surprise.

After Ma had died, she'd kept waiting for Pa to give her the inheritance Ma had said she'd set aside just for her. But when she'd asked him, he'd simply chewed on his tobacco and said nothing. She'd planned on using that money to get herself situated somewhere besides in the logging camp. But from Pa's lack of response, it was clear she'd have to find another way.

"Thank you for the recipe, Ruth." If she started out with one Tom really hated, then she'd have sent him a message about what she thought of his challenge.

"Mine are all gone." Sven patted his stomach.

The pretty blonde blushed. "Thank you, Sven."

She turned aside and whispered to Jo, "This is supposed to help you, not me." When the girl sighed, Mrs. Peyton shook her head.

Blue, right up under the big Swede's feet, wagged his tail to beat the band, begging for a treat. Jo tossed him half of a dried up biscuit. He leapt up and caught it mid-air, then slumped onto the floor with a loud thump.

Pearl waved her wooden spoon. "We'll make sure Jo beats Tom at his own game—you'll see."

Jo searched her heart. She wanted to embarrass Tom by turning him down. She had no intention of marrying a lumberjack and continuing this life. She had taken over her mother's job to help her father. But it'd been months now. And she'd just borrowed her friend's recipe not to help procure herself a husband, but to aggravate him. She needed to apologize to Ruth and tell her the real reason she'd used the old-fashioned recipe. Of course it hadn't helped that she'd also used up their oldest stock of dried fruit and nuts.

But a sudden thought flashed through her mind. What if Tom loved this cake? What if, when he learned it was Ruth's, he said she won the challenge? Picturing pretty blonde Ruth with handsome Tom made Jo's stomach churn.

She wanted out of the kitchen, which suddenly felt too crowded. "I have to go sit down in the back and make up my shopping list for town. Anything you all want to add?"

"Vanilla," Irma called out.

Mrs. Peyton stopped mashing potatoes. "Lots of sugar, both brown and white if they have it, and plenty of molasses, too."

"Cardamom, cinnamon, ginger, nutmeg, and mace." Ruth blinked her pretty blue eyes.

Pearl pulled a scrap of paper out of her pocket and handed it to Jo. "Oats, oat bran, wheat flour, rye, and corn meal—fresh ground from that mill by the river. You'll need to go there and please do not get it from Mr. Cooper at the store—his is old."

Jo tucked the slip of paper into her apron pocket. "It seems to me, ladies, that you only have one thing on your mind."

Irma nodded. "Making more fruitcake."

Sven looked up from carefully pouring kerosene. "I think you will have to try another recipe." He had a look on his face that he always got when he had a secret. Had Tom already announced the whole thing was a prank?

Pearl wrapped an arm around Ruth, whose face had fallen. "Now Ruth, lest you think we don't believe your recipe to be a winner, I want you to consider—who, of all those big strappin' men—do you wish to please with your baking?"

The young woman looked down at her boots, just as worn as Jo's. "Not Tom."

Tears filled her eyes as she turned and hugged Jo, her head barely reaching her shoulder. She whispered, "I want Sven to make me an offer like Tom made you."

Relief coursed through Jo. Tomorrow when she went to town, she'd get everything she needed to make the best fruitcake ever.

Tom trailed the other lumberjacks into the cook building. He was in such a jolly mood from sleeping in his new bunk that he didn't mind being last in line. And if he wasn't mistaken, he smelled something sweet—cake.

As she served him, Pearl leaned over and whispered to Tom, "Where can I get my hands on your mother's recipe?"

Tom chuckled. His mother would never surrender her prized "fruitcake receipt", handed down for generations.

"Miss Pearl, I apologize, but she'll hand that recipe over her cold dead body and maybe not even then."

The older lady's eyes widened. Jo turned from the huge black stove, holding a tray of muffins. The unmistakable scent of fruit and spices emanated from the baked goods. She offered a tight smile.

"Mr. Jeffries, you might want to try a sample of our fruitcake."

"Fruitcake in November?" He inhaled deeply. "Looks like you want to make sure you get plenty of opportunities in case you fail. Good planning on your part, Miss Christy."

Jo scowled at him, her wooden spoon now held like a scepter in her capable hands.

He quirked his eyebrows at her and her lips twitched as though fighting a smile. "Not that I am complaining, mind you."

"You better not be." Pearl laughed.

The scent of Christmases from long ago ran through his mind. His sister being courted by the man who would become her husband. He and his brother flanking Mama and Papa at the church services after Rebecca had wed. Mama slicing out thick slabs of fruitcake and covering them with creamy custard sauce. His mouth watered. The Christmas tradition of fruitcake was one of his favorites.

"Yes, ma'am, I'd welcome a try." He reached for a muffin but she made a threatening gesture with the wood spoon.

Jo Christy fluttered her eyelashes and bobbed a curtsey. "Why, Mr. Jeffries—have you had time to get to town to procure a ring already?"

His mouth dropped open. He wanted that fruitcake badly and he didn't want to offend the beautiful young lady who'd captured his heart.

"I have an heirloom that might suffice." If she didn't mind it being a rusted horseshoe nail ring he'd made for Rebecca, and returned to him by his brother-in-law after her death, along with a trinket box full of gifts he'd given his sister over the years—ear bobs and such.

"Well then—here you go." She placed a muffin on his plate, to the side of the turnips, mashed potatoes, gravy, and roast pork that covered the rest.

What had he gotten himself into? Tom headed to the Christy's table, where he'd been invited—or rather ordered—to sit. Maybe that was why he didn't mind being last in line.

Boss Christy inclined his head toward a seat between Ox and Moose, but the two men had pushed their seats in on the vacant wooden chair so that it was lodged too tightly between them for Tom to get in. A slow burn began in his gut.

He leaned forward. "Gentlemen, give way so I can sit down." He slid his plate onto the unvarnished pine table. Seemed strange, after growing up in a house full of Mother's antiques, to use furniture that would likely be thrown in a fire as soon as the place logged out.

When the two men continued to eat, Mr. Christy set down his fork. Tom hated to do it, but these two young men were acting like recalcitrant schoolboys. His action wouldn't *hurt* Ox and Moose, but it would get results. He wedged his thumbs down into a tender spot on their necks. Both yipped and Jo's black lab popped out from beneath the table, giving a mournful howl.

Mr. Christy laughed and waved for Tom to sit, as his two sons pulled their chairs apart and Tom took his place between them. Their ruddy cheeks looked just as embarrassed as the tough boys in Ohio he'd had to convince to behave after numerous warnings.

The boss winked at him. "Welcome, son."

Son? Had the camp owner just approved him? As a professor, his father had saved that term only for his favorite students—the ones he'd bring home to visit at the farm. Tom swallowed hard. What had started as a bit of fun with Josephine had become complicated by her family's involvement.

He closed his eyes, bowed his head and said a blessing over his meal. *Dear Lord, may I survive this meal and the Christy men and know what to do about that beautiful Christy woman up front. Amen.*

Blue Dog licked Tom's leg. As was their custom, wherever Tom found him, he slipped him a little bite of his food. In this case, the muffin Jo had made—its texture so hard he feared he might lose a tooth if he bit into it.

Moose elbowed him. "Saw you do that."

On his other side, Ox palmed his dessert and passed it to the dog, too.

Mr. Christy scowled. "A fair bet is a fair bet." He buttered his muffin and brought it to his lips.

"You know about it, Pa?" Ox asked around a mouthful of turnips. "About the fruitcake challenge?"

"Pa!" Jo hurried toward the table, her hands clutching a massive bowl of whipped potatoes. "Don't eat that muffin."

Ruth followed her, placing a platter of sliced pork by her employer. "I'm so sorry ... but Mother's cake ... it—it's meant to be dipped into your coffee first."

The big man plunked half of the muffin in his blue and white enamelware cup.

"Hold it there for a minute." Ruth chewed her lower lip as she looked first at Mr. Christy and then to the other end of the table, where Sven lifted his complete muffin out of his coffee mug and set it back onto his plate, coffee flowing from every crevice onto the plate.

Sven pulled back from the table, stood, turned and clasped his hand to his chest. "*Det är bra.* It's good, Ruth. Just like my mother made. Let it swim in the good strong coffee first. " The cacophony of men slurping, banging utensils, and laughing ceased as the blond man whistled.

Sven raised his arms. "If you want to keep what's left of your teeth you need to soak *den goda fruktkaka*—your good fruitcake before you eat."

Color drained from Ruth's face. Jo plunked the bowl of potatoes in front of Ox and then moved to Ruth's side, taking her elbow.

A grin split the Swede's face as he swiveled back toward Ruth. She had tears rolling down her cheeks and his tawny eyebrows rose. He cleared his throat and faced the men again. "Tom Jeffries isn't the only man to issue a Fruitcake Challenge this winter. I declare that Ruth has made a cake just like *my* mother's and, if she'll have me, I'll marry her this spring!"

The hall erupted in hoots, hollers, and Frenchman's caps being thrown in the air. Sven ran to Ruth, picked her up and swirled her around in the air.

"Yes!" she cried out.

Tom frowned. Would Jo shed tears of joy if he claimed her fruitcake the best ever? His eyes found her as she patted at the moisture on her face then turned and strode through her calico skirts toward the kitchen.

Had Jo lied to him? *Was* she in love with Sven and he'd never acted on his feelings for her? Tom stared at his plate of food, wanting to toss the contents and leave the table, but Ox nudged him and pointed to his father.

Mr. Christy's obsidian eyes met Tom's. "Mr. Jeffries, I need a favor of you tomorrow."

"Sir?"

"You're gonna take my daughter into town to get supplies." He pulled a note sheet from his pocket and handed it to Ox, who passed it to Tom.

On it was written a monetary amount. "Sir?"

"Make sure she doesn't exceed that budget for our food supplies."

Moose pressed in and whispered. "She ain't good at figures."

The woman had a fine figure, but Tom knew her brother meant that Jo had difficulties with ciphering and sums. "I'll bring an accounting book with me, sir, if you wish."

The man nodded curtly then resumed eating his mashed potatoes. Tom followed suit, lost in his thoughts of Jo pining over Sven.

Mr. Christy pulled a newspaper out from inside his wool shirt and tapped at a headline. "Price of fruit has gone up."

Chapter 5

The two dray horses bobbed their heads as though trying to decide if they'd let Pa's choice of driver take the reins. Today, toothless Mr. Brevort wouldn't drive—Tom would. Jo pulled her coat more tightly around her body as a gust of wind spiraled dirt up from the ground.

Her father, still handsome at forty-six, possessed a full head of dark curls, flashing black eyes, and the muscular build of a man half his age. He patted the horses and murmured encouragement to them as Tom came around to where Jo stood, on the side.

"Up you go." Tom lifted Jo onto the wagon as though she were a sack of down.

Before she could thank him, he'd turned, pulled a folded woolen blanket from a nearby tree stump and draped it across her lap. He handed her another folded blanket.

"In case it gets any chillier."

Pa nodded in approval. "If you're not back by dinner I'll send my boys looking for you."

"Thank you, sir." Tom climbed up onto the seat beside her, the wagon creaking in protest.

Did he actually *just thank* Pa for threatening to send her brothers after them?

Tom displayed a pistol. "You can't be too careful out in these woods, sir."

Pa walked around to her side of the wagon and handed Jo the zippered cash bag as a black flash of fur exited the cook shack and ran straight toward them.

When Blue's attempts to launch himself up onto the wagon failed, Pa gave him a lift and in two shakes of his tail, Blue had settled himself beside Jo, nudging her closer to Tom with his head. Her cheeks warmed.

Her father raised and lowered his index finger, motioning her to move farther over on the seat and right against Tom's strong shoulder. She pulled the blanket from beneath her pet as his tail slapped the wooden floorboard in glee.

"You have enough room, Miss Christy?" His eyebrows rose in question over eyes that shone deeper green today, like the pines surrounding them. Pines that would soon be logged out and sent off to the mills to be made into homes and grand hotels like those on nearby Mackinac Island. While she was in town today, she'd look to see if they had need of help at the train station restaurant, where many travelers disembarked on their way to the island.

"I'm fine." She tucked the blanket in around her, hoping that would give her enough room so she wouldn't be pressed up against him the entire trip to and from the hour's drive to town.

They headed out to the road and soon rocked on through the countryside, Tom guiding the horses around ruts. "Beautiful out here, isn't it, Miss Christy?"

She'd never been seated so close to someone who wasn't her own kin. This near she could see the fine lines framing Tom's eyes. "How old are you?"

His hands jerked on the reins, startling the horses, but he regained control. "Twenty-eight. Why do you ask?"

"Why haven't you married?" The words flew out of her mouth. Overhead birds chattered as though scolding her for asking.

He blew out a long puff of breath that clouded in the chill air. "I almost did, once. I waited four long years for my fiancée to finish her schooling."

Jo looked down at her hands, their chafed skin covered in mittens today.

"She wanted to be a doctor."

She gasped. "A doctor?"

His challenge to her truly had been a joke. No man who'd set his heart on marrying a modern educated woman would marry up with a camp cook. Disappointment battled with relief over ending this game Tom was playing.

"What happened?"

He redirected his gaze ahead. "Received a better offer."

"Lumber camps aren't a good choice for lady docs." As far as she knew there weren't too many of them and those who'd finished their training tended to go to the big cities, where people were more open to newfangled notions.

He chuckled. "I wasn't a lumberjack."

"What were you, then?" She chewed her lower lip. All those big words he used. The way he scolded the shanty boys when they were out of line. His after dinner stories read to the camp children.

"A minion."

"Minion?" She didn't want to ask what that meant.

"I was someone who had to dance to the tune of a board of men who had no idea what was involved in my work—unlike your father, who does. He has the respect of the men."

A board. A school board, perhaps? *A teacher.* She'd heard Moose's friend, Myra, a schoolteacher in town complain about the requirements. The woman couldn't so much as sneeze without accounting for her actions. If her suspicions were right, Moose wanted to marry the pretty teacher.

"So that's why you became an axman?"

His face reddened. "After my father died, I needed to make better wages to help my mother keep our home. Her family has owned the property for a hundred years or better. They earned the hundred acres for fighting in the American Revolution."

"Oh." What could she say to that? Ma's family and Pa's populated the hills of Kentucky. Maybe they, too, had earned their property during the Great War for Independence. Regardless, Granny didn't want Pa staying there for some reason and kept funding his lumbering efforts with money from the family stores. So they'd moved on from place to place ever since she was ten.

Sitting beside Tom, a yearning for permanence took root in Jo. Regardless of the outcome of his challenge, he'd been scorned once by a woman. Surely as a Christian she shouldn't humiliate him. Not like she'd planned.

She moistened her lips. "What will you do when this camp closes out?"

"I don't know. What about you?"

"I'm not going on. I know that. But I've got to find a job and … and let my Pa know."

Beside her, Blue began to yip as he tried to scramble up to sitting.

Movement in the tree line caught her eye. Tom followed her gaze. He reached inside his coat and retrieved his gun.

Overhead, the sun dimmed as thick clouds bunched together.

"Jo—you able to take the reins?"

She grasped them as several men, in tattered clothes, stumbled toward the road. "Hee-yah!" She slapped the reins against the horses and they pulled the empty cart faster down the lane.

Tom fired off a warning shot as the men ran toward them. Jo didn't look back, but Blue barked furiously. She couldn't let go of the reins and if she grabbed her dog now, he'd bolt. *Dear God don't let him run off after those men.*

Tom fired again. "Threw up some dirt at them, Jo. They're rubbing their eyes."

He grabbed the reins back and Jo wrapped an arm around Blue. The dog continued to pant loudly and whine as the team carried them at a brisk pace out to the main road that led to town.

Jo's heart beat so fast she could scarcely get her breath.

When Tom slowed the wagon and pulled her close, she didn't resist. Instead, she rested her head on his shoulder while Blue slumped down, covering her feet.

"It'll be all right, Josephine." Reins in one hand, Tom patted her pet's head. "Don't you worry."

After Tom and Jo had dropped Blue Dog off at the miller's, they'd continued on to town. Now, what seemed like hours later, Tom prayed their procurements at the mercantile had ceased. After totaling the figures, Tom surmised that Jo's purchases resulted in a sum well over the allotted budget. She'd just tried on a pair of lady's boots but had put them back on the display shelf after she'd looked at the price.

When she moved on to the yard goods, he slipped over to the rack, grabbed the footwear, and then brought them to the sales clerk.

"Box these up separate, please," he said, keeping his voice low. "Put them on my tab."

"Yessir. Didn't realize Miss Christy had a beau." The young sales clerk's long straight hair flopped into his eyes as he bent and almost reverently tucked the brown boots inside a cardboard box, covered it, and then wrapped twine around it. "Was thinking about asking her father if I could come visit her out to the camp sometime."

"Well, don't," Tom ground out between clenched teeth. What had gotten into him? Maybe those tramps on the road had him riled up. Or maybe it was the way Jo felt tucked next to him, her soft body conforming to his as they rode into town.

The young man's pale blue eyes met his and widened. "No, sir. I can see right away that she's your gal."

His gaze flitted to Jo, whom Tom caught staring at him in what appeared to be open admiration. She twirled so fast toward the bolts of cloth that she knocked half a dozen over.

"Excuse me." The young clerk moved toward the display, but Tom stepped in front of him.

"I've got this." He came alongside Jo, whose cheeks flushed pink, which heightened her prettiness. Her deep auburn hair and hazel eyes contrasted nicely.

Tom's hands brushed against her as they both bent to pick up a bolt of cheerful green and red cotton fabric. He felt a spark move through him, igniting a longing that this Christmas could be as festive as the fabric—a time filled with happy new memories.

"I got distracted." Jo averted her gaze and straightened the cloth. "Can I get that bolt of Christmas cloth? It would look so merry on the tables."

"I don't see why not." Except that she'd already exhausted every bit of money her father had allotted … and then some.

He brought the fabric to the front and motioned for the clerk to incline his head. "Go ahead and total out the order, but anything over this amount…" He handed the man Mr. Christy's note. "Put that on my account with the boots."

"But it's quite a fair amount over with this cloth, Mister."

Tom held up his hand. "Please, just do as I say."

They'd not even stopped at the mill yet. What would *that* total be? Tom opened his wallet and examined the contents. As Mr. Christy had suspected, fruit prices—even on dried fruit that would have been harvested the previous year—had already risen. Prices were already inflated in this area because of the long trip most food took to arrive there. Hopefully flour prices were stable.

Jo and Tom shopped along the main street for personal items while Mr. Cooper's men filled the wagon with their order. She'd brought a large bag of her sugar cookies and spent time trading with some of the Chippewa.

"I need something for Ruth for Christmas." She held aloft a blue beaded necklace, then made a trade.

They walked on and she stopped at a restaurant, at the train station, and at a druggist to inquire about work. She'd also stopped at the post office, where jobs from southern Michigan and even the Upper Peninsula were posted. With each address Jo recorded in her tiny notepad, his heart sank. But if, like Mother, she wanted to work then perhaps he could return to teaching. Still, he wanted to be able to support a wife on his own. Or, was that his pride speaking? Biblical admonitions came to mind, warning him that humility was a virtue and pride a sin.

Everywhere they stopped, people hugged Jo and asked about her mother. And, each time, she cried. He bought an extra handkerchief for her at the mercantile when his became too soggy to be effective. When a stiff wind blew down from the straits, she allowed him to drape his arm around her.

Now, an hour later, as they rolled up toward the mill, Tom estimated the amount of money he'd need to pay for the various grains they'd need for the camp. He'd already sent his mother money for taxes. Her curt reply in her recent letter wasn't at all the appreciative missive he'd hoped for. Instead, she reiterated her plan to take up work as a businesswoman of sorts. *I've got a lot of life left in me, Thomas, and I intend to make my own way,* she'd written.

After securing the horses, Tom assisted Jo down and Blue came bounding from beneath the shade of an oak tree. "Good boy." He picked up a stick and threw it for the dog while Jo went to check on her order.

In a short while she returned, grinning. An impish gleam lit her eyes. "I'm done." She pointed back to massive sacks of milled wheat, cornmeal, oats, and rye.

Lord what have I got myself into here? The miller stopped the millstone from turning, wiped his hands, and headed toward Tom as his assistant swept up.

"Them shanty boys gonna eat good this month."

On Tom's coin, too. He bit his lower lip. When the man named the total, Tom clenched his jaw and reached for his wallet.

Jo frowned and watched as he pulled the money out and handed it to the man. When the proprietor failed to exchange the usual pleasantries, Tom offered his own.

"Thank you, sir, for doing business with us." Tom extended his hand.

"Oh, yes…" The miller smiled and shook hands. "Mighty fine to meet you, too."

He tucked the bills into the front of his white apron then waved his assistant over. The two men hoisted up a fifty-pound sack on each shoulder. Tom did the same, trailing Jo out to the wagon.

Tom cleared his throat. "We encountered some miscreants on the road on our way here."

The miller loaded his bags in the wagon with a resounding *thunk*. His assistant followed suit, flour dust puffing out from the bags.

"Don't know anybody by that name, Mister."

Jo gave Tom a pointed look. "He means we had trouble with some bums on the road near town."

"Oh." The miller scratched his balding pate. "Were there three of them?"

"Yes," Jo and Tom answered in unison.

"They stole from us yesterday and we chased them off." The miller's assistant squared his scrawny shoulders.

"I had to fire at them."

"Me, too." The owner pointed back toward the mill. "I always keep my shotgun ready, being situated out from town this far."

Jo shivered. Tom needed to get her home.

"I don't want a repeat on the way back but I'm prepared." He'd purchased additional ammunition for their return.

The miller whistled long and low. "Can't imagine what the Christy men would do to them fellas if they harmed this little lady."

Jo's features pinched together.

"I got Miss Christy here safely and I'll get her home again—safe."

Blue looked up from the bowl of water he'd noisily slurped from.

"Come, Blue," Jo called.

The retriever shook his black head and trotted over, but headed to Tom, not Jo.

She narrowed her eyes at him as Tom hoisted the good dog up and onto the floorboard.

"My own dog likes you better than he likes me." Her voice, so childlike and soft, stirred his protective nature.

"No, he doesn't, Josephine. He just knows I have treats in my pocket." Tom took Jo into his arms. He'd been about to lift her up but having her this close, with the scent of the rosewater she'd dabbed on at the store, intoxicating his senses. He could only stand and look at her changeable eyes, her perfectly straight nose, and then those tempting lips of hers. Lips that trembled. Lips inviting him to...

"Mr. Jeffries?" Her eyes had turned hard. "I believe you were going to help me up. Or did you injure yourself lifting the bags?"

Tom heaved her up then marched around to his side of the wagon. What had he been thinking? And with the miller and his helper right there?

Once he took his seat, he whistled for Blue, gave him a dried biscuit, and then motioned for the dog to perch between himself and Jo. He didn't need to be any closer to the pretty woman than he already was.

Jo spread her blanket around herself as the lab lay at their feet, between them. Tom directed the horses out onto the main road. For a few minutes they rode in silence. But when Jo spread the second blanket over his knees, he almost jumped.

"You all right, Tom?" She looked up. "Flakes are coming down. We'll need that extra blanket."

Light snowfall danced in the chill breeze. "Once we get into the woods we'll get less precipitation."

Beside him, she shivered. "Do you think those men will be there?"

"Let's pray not."

"Do you pray, Tom?"

"Every night. Don't you?"

"I do."

But were they praying for the same thing? Or were their prayers at odds with each other?

The next day, Jo woke with Pa well before sunrise and made sure he headed over to the kitchen shack for his breakfast. What a treat to be able to go back to bed and enjoy the warmth of quilts stitched by her mother, grandmother, and aunts. She could almost feel the love that had gone into making them. Ma used to let her sleep in and come to help with clean up after breakfast and to make sure the lunches were made up to be taken out to the men in the woods. In return, Jo had also worked the after dinner cleaning crew so Ma could spend some time at home with Pa. But that was before she got too sick to do much more than rock in Granny's rocking chair, wrapped in the very quilt covering Jo now.

As she lay beneath the covering, she replayed the conversations she and Tom had had on the way home. They'd talked about so many things that she couldn't remember them all. One thing she did recollect, though, was the way he made her feel—like she was the most special woman in the world. He listened to her concerns. He shared his trials as a teacher but also the joy he felt in watching a child learn to read and write. She sucked in a long slow breath, recollecting how good his arm felt, wrapped around her to keep her warm.

Someone rapped at Jo's window and she startled. She lifted her red gingham checkered curtain and peered out into the dark. A lamp illuminated Sven's blond mane and rugged features.

"Can I come in, Jo?"

"Sure—come on." She got up and slipped her arms into her robe and her feet into a pair of fur-lined moccasins.

She unhooked the lock and opened the door. Sven entered, with the usually foul-tempered Mr. Schmidt behind him. She closed the door.

"What brings you here?"

Sven brought down the shotgun from over the door and placed it on the table, in the main room's center. "Those men marched right into the kitchen pretty as you please, yesterday."

Jo gasped.

"*Ja*, Thomas told us you saw them on the road." The German man stomped, wiping his feet on the mat and Blue Dog rose from his bed to join them.

"Did they hurt anybody?"

"*Nein*, that relief cook, Irma, grabbed the shotgun in the corner and ran them off. She's the *fraulein* for me, I think." Mr. Schmidt waggled his bushy eyebrows. "Asked her to bake *me* a *gut* fruitcake."

"Irma?" The widow was such a quiet hard-working woman.

"*Ja*. She told them to git—just like you tell your dog when he's bad."

Sven removed his cap. "Your Pa didn't want to frighten you last night, so he didn't tell you. Tom slept outside your shack, I was at Ruth's in the middle of camp, and your brothers guarded each end of camp."

"Thomas has eaten and he is to sleep now, *ja*?" Mr. Schmidt rocked back and forth in his heavy boots, the floorboards creaking.

Sven yawned. "I'm gonna join him and your brothers for a snooze in the bunk house."

"I better get dressed then." Jo pulled her robe more tightly around her.

"Those tramps said they came for the teacher." Sven rubbed his bristly jaw. "Problem is—your brothers say they might have meant Tom. And you know poor excuse of a schoolteacher, Mr. Arnold, doesn't come into camp. So we'll need to talk with him today."

Chapter 6

Late November

No work for him today. The bunkhouse had never been so empty—
or so lonely. Recovered now from a brief bout of the ague, Tom rose
from his bunk and quickly dressed—the chill of November winds
rattling the windows in their frames. He'd go check on Ruth, too,
who had suffered from the same illness—both of them missing out
on the Thanksgiving feast. Not that either of them could have kept it
down. Today, he'd missed breakfast and his chance to get a glimpse
of Jo. Truth be told, her indifference during his illness cut him
deeply. But her brothers said if she stepped in that bunkhouse to
check on him, that she'd never have heard the end of it—especially
since he'd issued his fruitcake challenge. Camp driver, elderly
Frenchie Brevort said she didn't come feed him broth herself
because then the men would claim she was buttering him up for his
mother's fruitcake recipe. So, maybe she wasn't indifferent, but
afraid. But true love—God's love—cast out fear.

Right?

After washing his face at the pitcher and basin stand, Tom dried
off with a clean cloth. The scent of castile soap reminded him of
Jo—the way it clung to her unlike the sweat that permeated the
bunkhouse. Today, instead of work boots, he slipped his feet into
lined moccasins that Jo had insisted he needed and set off down the
pine-needle strewn trail toward Ruth's cabin. She might need a hand
with something, what with her father out at the logging site and all
those sisters to care for. They loved listening to his stories and the
youngest—six-year-old Amanda—was learning to read primers. Of
course her teacher may have had something to do with that, too, but
Tom liked to think his reading with the children had helped.

Tom approached Ruth's door, drawing his collar closed around
his neck to keep out the wind. A tiny blonde whirlwind flew out,
dressed only in a nightgown. Amanda shrieked when she saw him
and then covered her mouth.

The little girl tilted her head back to stare up at him. "I thought you were that bad man, Mr. Tom."

"Nope." Tom knelt on one knee, bringing him face-to-face with the child and pulled her close to shield her from the wind. "What bad man do you mean?"

She cupped her hands around her mouth and whispered in Tom's ear. "Go to the school and see."

A shiver worked his way up his back. Did she mean the teacher? They'd still had no word if the vandals on the road were seeking Arnold.

Ruth appeared in the doorway, her cheeks pink with health.

Rising, Tom pulled Amanda up with him and she wrapped her arms around his neck. "You look like you're feeling better, Ruth."

"Yes, thank God." She exhaled a huge sigh. "But Mandy won't go to school today."

Hadn't his father said all children complained about their schoolmasters? But Tom's students hadn't. Rather it was he who chafed at the saintly requirements he had to keep. Because he'd not been able to find a position in his own community, he'd been forced to take a position elsewhere, which meant he had to board with one of his student's families. At least he'd had his own room, albeit usually in a frigid attic. And he'd had to obtain permission to even take a weekend away to visit his mother. He'd not chafed at the rules about attending church because he firmly believed God had called him to be a teacher. And since he didn't smoke nor drink spirits, he'd had no difficulty with *that* rule. Since he was already engaged, he'd been given some leniency when Eugenia had come to visit. But after she'd discarded him like a spent bucketful of ash, the school board treated him differently, questioning his every move. It had become intolerable, and he'd felt that God's blessing on his profession had been lifted. Additionally, the low wages were insulting. Maybe Mr. Arnold also struggled with similar constraints, although Mr. Christy seemed to be quite lenient in oversight. Nothing about the little contact Tom had with the teacher seemed to suggest that Arnold perceived God's call on his work, though. If anything, the man seemed downright antsy whenever faith was mentioned.

Amanda tugged at his hand. "Promise me you'll go."

The men were already out at the site, well beyond here. They were so deep in the woods he'd not be joining them this day.

"I'll go."

She pulled again. "Right now?"

He exhaled a puff of air that caused the child's bangs to ripple on her rounded doll-like forehead. "All right."

Tom stood and wiped his hands on his pants. "I'll drop back by later."

"Thanks, Tom." Ruth took her sister's hand and led her back to a rudimentary bench made of smaller tree stumps topped by a board that rested against the side of the cabin.

His gut rumbled as he cut through the pine needle strewn path toward the makeshift schoolhouse. The square building resembled the family cabins but was situated farther into the woods. Smoke puffed from the short chimney. The door swung open and Mr. Arnold pulled Ruth's sister, Gretchen, by her long blond braid to the side of the structure. In his right hand, he held what looked like a leather whip. So intent was he on his task, that he didn't notice Tom standing there.

"Bend over!" the schoolmaster barked at the cowering girl.

Through the open school door, Tom spied the children's mortified faces. He ran toward the man just as Arnold raised the whip and grabbed it from his hand.

"Why, you!" Arnold whirled on him, his countenance dark with rage.

Gretchen's tear-streaked face reflected fear and relief.

"You interfering, barbarian! I am the schoolmaster here." Arnold lunged toward Tom.

When he raised his fist, Tom punched him in his gut, bringing the monster to his knees in the dank earth. The children swarmed from the schoolhouse.

Tom gave Gretchen a quick hug before turning to the other children. "Who else has been hurt by the teacher?"

They all glanced at each other. One by one they clustered around Tom.

"I told Papa," Gretchen whispered. "But he didn't believe me. Thank you for coming, Mr. Tom."

Arnold stood and pointed behind Tom. "They'll kick you out of the camp, you fool. Who do you think you are, coming in here and stirring up trouble?"

Tom heard the rustle of dried leaves beneath large feet and turned to see Ox and Moose amble out from the woods. What were they doing back so early? When the two brawny brothers got to the schoolhouse they paused, both of them tucking their thumbs into their red suspenders.

Arnold took three steps toward them. "This shanty boy just punched me."

Ox spit a wad of tobacco juice just past Arnold. "That true, Tom?"

"Yes, it is."

Gretchen ran to Moose. "Teacher was gonna whip me and Mr. Tom didn't let him."

Tom bent, retrieved the leather whip and displayed it for the brothers, knowing full well that if they let this man keep teaching he didn't want to be part of this camp. His stomachache rallied again, and churned within him.

Ox raised a hand to shield his eyes from the sun and appeared to stare straight ahead at Tom and the teacher. "You're relieved of duty."

Arnold smirked at Tom. "What did I tell you?"

Moose moved forward and grabbed the back of the brute's neck. "Not him—*you*! You're out of here! *Now*, Arnold."

The brothers linked arms with the man. "Besides, we think your true name might be Arnault, not Arnold, and that the police in Traverse City have reason to want to talk with you."

They bodily hauled him away from the school and toward the camp.

Gretchen wrapped her arms around Tom as a gust of wind sent dead leaves scurrying. "What are we gonna do about school, Mr. Tom?"

Inside her cabin, on a brief respite from kitchen work, Jo bent over the washing bucket by the window, scrubbing her good dress, readying it for church. She prayed Tom would be well enough to sit beside her again. Last week, she'd prayed the entire time that he'd cover her hand with his or hold her hand during the brief service. She'd watched him tap his fingers on his knee and then creep his fingers closer to her, but then he'd stop, clasp his hands together and stare intently at the preacher. She sighed at the recollection. At least he'd offered his arm on the way back to her cabin. And Pa allowed him to sit with them and chat during the lunch meal. What a blessing to have yet another new cook, Mrs. Lehto, a pretty brunette widow in her forties, to help so Jo could have a respite.

She rinsed out her dress, which needed to dry. Tomorrow night she would starch and press it. She looked through the window and spied Ruth as she ran across the clearing, looking well and like herself again.

The younger woman tapped on the door and then came inside. "Jo—guess what? Tom stopped Mr. Arnold from hurting Gretchen."

"What?" Jo dropped her dress back into the rinse water and rose.

"That's all I know. Come on outside." Ruth turned and went back out. Jo grabbed a heavy shawl and followed her out into the cold breeze. At least this year the winter was beginning mild.

Emerging from the tree line, Jo's brothers practically dragged the schoolteacher over the dirt yard and then past her and Ruth. With a black eye and a split lip, the teacher appeared to have been pummeled.

Cringing, Jo watched with Ruth from the stoop. They wrapped arms around each other as a gust of wind carried dirt up from the hard-packed ground.

"Miss Christy," the man croaked as he passed. Blood dripped down his chin and the front of his cream-colored shirt.

Moose jerked the man forward. "She ain't gonna help save your worthless hide when she hears what you did."

Stiffening, Jo wiped her hands on her apron. "What happened?"

Ox spat into a little patch of brown grass. "Tom caught him about to whip Gretchen and he stopped him."

Teachers had been known to take a rod to misbehaving pupils. Had Tom overreacted?

"Tom did *what*?" How could he have beaten up the schoolmaster?

Ruth linked her arm through Jo's and leaned in. "Sven says his real name is Arnault, not Arnold, and he's wanted by the sheriff in Traverse City."

"What?" Had this man harmed other children? What had this Mr. Arnold or Arnault done?

"Those men who came to camp were part of his gang." Ox's dark eyes flashed in anger. "That's what the sheriff thinks."

"Pa!" Moose called out as they pulled the man toward the office shack.

Ruth's sisters raced across the clearing, so close together as they ran that their calico skirts swished against each other's. None wore their coats. Jo cupped her hands around her mouth. "Come over here, girls."

Gretchen panted as she stopped before Jo. "Mr. Tom saved me."

Wrapping an arm around Gretchen and Amanda, Jo pulled them into the cabin as Ruth followed with her sister, Edith. After serving them hot cocoa and sugar cookies, Jo played a game of charades with them all. Jo's favorite was twelve-year-old Edith's portrayal of Tom as a banty rooster, strutting about the cabin and then pointing at Jo, then back at herself and winking. Ruth had burst into laughter and called out, "That's Tom."

Jo had laughed, too, but recently she'd seen the godly man Tom could be, as she'd spent time with him. And his braggart ways had lessened. Still, he'd not affirmed that any of the fruitcakes she'd concocted were worthy of him.

Bidding the girls goodbye, Jo couldn't shake the image of Mr. Arnold's bloody face from her mind. Pa and Tom had accompanied the accused man into town. If Tom could be so violent with his fellow man…the thought gave her pause. Now she understood why Pa and her brothers kept constant vigil over her. Theirs was a family lumber camp with few single men. And as such they didn't have the fighting and brawling seen in some of the other places, such as a few they'd visited near Traverse City. Her tentative imaginings of a growing romance with Tom shook like geese wings as they prepared to take flight high above the pines. She was left feeling like the lonely loon who bobbed on the lake by herself, waiting, but never joined by her mate. Watching the bird, some nights, made Jo feel so sad, with an emptiness she'd not recognized until Tom had arrived in camp.

Why had he come? This ache in her heart was a burden she couldn't bear.

Jo retrieved the note from the bakeshop across the straits in St. Ignace. And she penned a hasty reply. She could take one of the railroad cars, pulled across by barge. With her savings, she'd have enough for the passage and at least a month's worth of supplies. The position came with room and board.

Now, to tell Pa.

Tom strode across the mucky yard in his heavy boots. In a box, tucked under his arm, were Arnold's punishment tools, including what looked like a cat of nine tails. Men like Arnold should be locked up forever.

He was almost to the Christy's cabin when Jo stepped in his path, her hair as fiery as her cheeks. "How could you?"

Tom pulled himself up to his full height. "He deserved it."

"To be beaten up like that?"

Tom pulled the box from beneath his arm and displayed a vicious looking horsewhip. "What do you think about this being cracked on a student's back?"

"He wouldn't…" Her pretty lips quivered as frosty air blew in across nearby Lake Michigan.

Longing to pull her into his arms, instead, he removed his mackinaw jacket and draped it over her shoulders.

Ox and Moose exited the office. "You got more of Arnault's stuff there, Tom?"

"Sure do."

"You're violent, too." Jo's low petulant words pierced him. She crossed her arms over her chest, pulling his coat tightly around her.

One punch to the gut? She thought his hit equated with a man who beat children? She was one mixed up lady. What kind of mother would she be if she allowed her children to be mistreated by someone like Arnold?

"I beg to disagree, ma'am."

Moose and Ox trudged toward them, both rubbing their fists. Ox had streaks of red on his knuckles. So did Moose. Apparently neither bothered to wash the so-called teacher's blood from their hands.

Tom snorted in disgust, understanding what had happened. He turned to Jo. "Let me guess. Did Mr. Arnold arrive back here with a busted up face?"

Jo glanced between Tom and her brothers. "You should know he did, Mr. Jeffries."

Ox gave a quick shake of his head and jerked his thumb toward Tom. "Nah, he didn't see it."

Moose placed himself between Jo and Tom and grabbed the box full of Arnold's disgusting paraphernalia. "You have no idea what kinda man would take out his frustration on a child using this stuff, Sis."

Ox smacked one fist into his palm. "He deserved what he got and if he had another face, I'd rearrange that one, too."

Jo's face went slack. She must have realized that her brothers had inflicted whatever damage Arnold sustained.

"We better wash up before dinner." Moose examined his fists, spitting on one and rubbing it against his thigh.

"But who is going to teach those children now?" Jo stepped forward and stomped her foot. He couldn't help smiling at the fact that she was wearing the boots he'd bought for her.

Although she didn't apologize to him for thinking he'd done the damage to Arnold's face, Jo was chewing her lower lip, which meant regrets might be forthcoming.

"Pa had a horrid time finding this supposed teacher."

"She's right." Moose frowned. "Pa couldn't get anybody but that bit of scum to come this far north."

"I can keep tutoring them at night." Tom had kept his agreement with the brothers, reading to the children every night and instructing those who struggled.

Jo rocked on the balls of her feet, her mouth fixed in a grim line of agitation. "What are the mothers supposed to do when part of the reason they agreed to stay in this camp was because we had a teacher?"

"Miss Christy…"

Moose raised his hand. "We had an agreement, Tom, and I expect you'll honor it."

"Proposition you accepted freely." Ox repeatedly flexed his fingers and then fisted them.

Tom got their message. But if he took over the teaching job, how was he to help his mother? He'd pulled in a good paycheck week after week. Was that to now end? And what would that mean for his chances with Jo?

With the whispering of the pines came a soft assurance from God—He had a plan for both of their lives.

Jo removed Tom's jacket and shoved it at him. "Thank you for the loan." Her tone of voice was anything but grateful and a muscle in his jaw twitched.

Crossing her arms, Jo ran back into her cabin.

Was the rumor true? Mr. Brevort had told him that the new bakeshop owner from St. Ignace sent inquiries to the merchants in Mackinaw City about Jo. Tom looked up at the quaking boughs of the pines in search of an answer. Surely God didn't plan for him to lose her when he'd only just realized what a treasure she was.

Chapter 7

December, 1890

Would the brand new bakeshop in St. Ignace have dainty curtains like Ma had made for her hope chest? Jo hoped the building looked like the white clapboard-sided pastry shop for sale in Mackinaw City. Maybe the owner was taking his business to the Upper Peninsula because of all the lumber camps opening up there. Patting the letter, with its offer for employment, Jo eyed the serving counter. The leftover fruitcake—one of Mrs. Peyton's recipes—seemed to taunt her from its perch. "Not good enough, not even close."

Another week closer to Christmas and still no fruitcake that Tom would approve. The previous evening, after dinner, Pa spent a long time talking with the handsome lumberjack, but Jo hadn't heard what they'd said. However, she had felt Pa's, Tom's, and her brothers' eyes on her as she and her ladies cleaned up. Afterward, Tom had walked her home, telling her stories about growing up in Ohio. Not that it mattered what she learned about him, since she obviously couldn't please the finicky man. Besides, she was most definitely getting out of the lumber camp.

She removed her apron. Would the one she'd wear at the bakery in the Upper Peninsula be pretty? She'd pull her pink calico floral print with ruffles from her cedar *hopeless* chest to wear if her employer allowed her to don the frilly garment for work.

Mrs. Peyton ceased chopping potatoes for pasties. "Jo, Frenchie's waiting."

Inhaling the pleasant co-mingling scents of beef pasties and sugar and vanilla, Jo turned from center of the kitchen. Today they were fully staffed. Even Irma came in to start doing some cooking ahead for the upcoming holidays. Thousands of cookies would be baked between now and Christmas.

Pearl paused in rolling out dough and looked up as Jo headed toward the back door. "I need some cocoa powder off that shipment, if'n you don't mind."

"Sure thing." She opened the door and shivered as the frosty lake breeze penetrated her threadbare dress.

Outside, Mr. Brevort sat high atop the buckboard. He directed his team to pull the dray as close to the back door as possible.

The horses tried to shake their heads but he held them steady and shouted at them in French, "*Arrêtez de tirer.*" Stop pulling.

They calmed.

"Most of the food goes inside, *mademoiselle.*" The elderly man stumbled beneath a burlap bag marked on the front in bold black letters—WALNUTS. He caught himself and adjusted his load. "Open the door for me, *s'il vous plait?*"

"Oh, yes." She did so and then went to the wagon to inspect his purchases.

She gasped when she spied crates of expensive dried fruit—cherries, apples, raisins, and dates. Tears pricked her eyes. The shanty boys had thrown in much money to help her continue to create her fruitcakes.

Pearl accompanied Mr. Brevort back out again. "Oh Frenchie, I'd love to try your recipe tonight—I have everything ready to go."

"*Merci.*" He grasped Pearl's flour-streaked hand and raised it to his lips. "And I would wager it would taste as good or better than my *maman's.*"

To Jo's amazement, Pearl blushed.

Later that night, after dinner, they served up Mr. Brevort's French variant of fruitcake. Ruth and the ladies served the slices to all the men. Once again, Tom was served last, coming to the front of the building and to Jo for his sample. As usual, she found her breath coming in short and difficult efforts whenever he was so near.

Mrs. Peyton pressed close to Jo, and whispered, "Tom's so handsome, what do you bet his mother's a French woman? This could be the cake that does the trick, Jo."

Passing the small tin plate of fruitcake to Tom, their fingers brushed and she felt the warmth of his touch. Her heartbeat sped up. He gave her a slow grin then plunged his fork into the cake and scooped out a large portion.

Waiting in rapt attention, she watched him lift the light and moist creation to his full lips. He winked at her and she felt heat creeping into her cheeks.

After he swallowed, he blinked. Then, he slowly shook his head, but Jo could see genuine remorse in his eyes. He shrugged. "I won't lie. It's the fruit in the cake—just doesn't taste as moist as what my mother used."

Jo knew he took the Word seriously. "The Good Book says don't lie, Tom, so I'll keep trying." Her voice sounded soft and decidedly feminine to her ears. This man was affecting her in strange ways.

"Thank you, Josephine. I admire a woman who perseveres."

Ruth leaned in and whispered, "Bible talks about persevering in trials and I'd say Tom is your trial."

Jo chuckled. He had been a trial and the man still frustrated her, but he'd grown on her.

"I better go sit down." Tom's emerald eyes captured hers. "But I'd like to walk you home later, if you're agreeable."

She nodded, wanting to feel his arm around her again, as he escorted her to the cabin.

Pa waved Jo over so she could sit and take her meal. Tonight Pa had directed Tom to sit at the table nearest the back door, and farthest from her. This was also where he read to the children at night after the men cleared out from dinner. She watched the bulging muscles in Tom's back strain against the checked fabric of his shirt as he headed up the narrow path between the tables, and then blinked away the sight as she went to her father's side.

"Have a seat, darlin'." He even stood and motioned for her brothers to do the same. From the end of the table, Mr. Brevort held his French fruitcake aloft, tears streaming down his pale cheeks and into his snowy beard. "*Plus parfait*—beyond perfection, Josephine and Pearl."

Patting her hair, Pearl slid in next to the man. Mr. Brevort covered her free hand with his. "*Merci beaucoup.* Thank you so much for your kindness to an old man."

"Pshaw, we're not that old, Frenchie. I bet you could still beat me at a game of checkers."

"You're on." He laughed.

Was it Jo's imagination or did they both have spots of red on their cheeks? Had this fruitcake challenge sparked yet another courtship?

She slid into her spot next to Pa and he and her brothers sat again, exhaling loudly as though the effort strained what few manners they'd recalled from Ma's instruction.

Pa said a quick blessing. When she looked up, his gaze locked with hers.

"Frenchie told me what it cost to fill those racks in the storeroom with all those jars of fruit."

Jo buttered her roll. "Pa, those men chipped in on the purchase of their own free will."

"Would you say it was about half of what you and Tom came home with?" The growl in his voice was worse than usual.

"Maybe." She kept her tone light. She was a twenty-five-year-old woman, not a child to be scolded.

His neck grew crimson above his red and black checked wool shirt. "Which means you couldn't have paid for that entire order I gave you without putting it on credit. And what have I told you about that before?"

Exhaling loudly, she set her roll on the edge of the blue and white speckleware plate. "We don't charge any items."

"That's right." He eyed her as he bit into his own roll.

Jo tugged at the cloth napkin on her lap.

"Sure am glad Tom came up with this idea." Moose reached in front of Jo and she leaned back to avoid getting whacked in the face as her brother passed a piece of the French fruitcake to their father.

When Jo glared at her brother and pushed his arm away, Moose just laughed.

Ox paused from filling his face. "We're getting our sweet tooth satisfied. That's for sure."

"Tom told me he made up the difference on the bill, Pa." Ox tossed another slice of cake in their father's direction and Pa caught it between his two beefy hands.

"He did what?" Jo mentally reviewed the items they'd purchased. Tom never said a word to her about the excess cost.

Pa's black eyebrows drew together into one dark line. "We'll talk about this later, Jo, and what it means. Your ma shoulda taught you better and Tom's ma, too."

"But I didn't know." Her protest was met with Pa's raised palm. She pressed the toes of her new boots together, ashamed that a man had purchased clothing for her. What if the others heard? Her brothers knew and their two big mouths combined might cause a problem. *No. They'd have thunked Tom on the head and warned him not to spread that information around.*

At the end of the table Mr. Brevort and Pearl whispered to one another, their heads nearly touching. Then Frenchie stood. When the lumberjacks failed to quiet down, Sven, seated at the next table with Ruth, whistled loudly. Then the Swede came around and hoisted the smaller man up onto a bench.

The Frenchman bowed. "I may not be a young *homme*—man—like Tom but I extend the same offer. Since Pearl has made a French fruitcake as good as Maman's and I will propose."

The woman flushed as she clasped her hands to her bosom. Jo stared, dizziness blurring her vision.

Moose leaned his flannel-covered shoulder into her. "We figure if Tom is offering to pay up then maybe he's serious. If you don't want his proposal, Sis, you can still play a good joke on the axe man."

"What do you mean?"

"Accept the same dare from the other men. Me and Ox could pay some of them like Irish Jack, Finlander Reino, and Scotty McNear to do the same bet."

She cringed. "I would never accept them—I've known them my entire life."

Moose shoveled a forkful of beef pasty into his mouth and grinned. Then he simply picked up the dough covered meat pie and ate it like a sandwich. Between bites, he said, "So? You could let them propose and then say no."

Wasn't that what she'd already planned to do to Tom? *Oh God, forgive me.* She'd grown to care for the man. Maybe he really did intend to honor his offer. But she'd just written her acceptance for the bakery job in the Upper Peninsula. She didn't want to be tied to a lumber camp nor to a man who worked in one. But Tom was so different from any man she'd even known. Of course she'd known manly men—they were lumberjacks. But Tom possessed a tenderness that made him seem like a masculine man who knew his own strength and how to restrain it.

After dinner, as she cleaned up with her helpers, Jo watched Tom reading to the children. And in turn, the older ones read sections aloud to the younger.

"Very good, Mandy." The tenderness in Tom's voice carried above the kitchen clatter.

Jo paused from scrubbing a pot and spied the little girl beaming as she clutched "The Adventures of Pinocchio" to her chest.

Mrs. Peyton came alongside her. "Isn't that sweet how Tom is with those young'uns?"

Raising her eyebrows, Jo nodded in agreement. "I bet he'd be a good father."

Oh my, had she really said that aloud? The older woman's chuckle affirmed that she had.

When the lesson and the cleaning were done, Sven and the parents arrived to accompany the children home. Mr. Brevort even returned for Pearl.

Tom helped Jo as they extinguished the last of the kerosene lamps, saving one to see by. He put on his mackinaw coat and then assisted her into her heavy wool cape, pulling the hood up over her head. His fingers brushed her cheeks then lingered on the sides of her neck, sending a shiver of delight through her.

His face grew thoughtful as he gazed down into her eyes. "It's starting to snow."

So that was why he'd done what had seemed like an intimate gesture, pulling up her hood. Sure enough, through the window she spied flakes of white floating down on gentle puffs of wind. Tom held the lantern aloft as they exited the building. Once outside, he cupped her elbow as he guided her toward home. Jo kept her head down, to prevent the icy wind from hitting her face. But when they reached her stoop, Tom gently pulled her hood back and placed two fingers beneath her chin.

She looked up into his face, the moonlight illuminating his fine features. "Jo, I think you are the finest woman I've ever known."

Now that simply wasn't true. Was he like Pinocchio? His comment was like icy water splashing her, colder than the wind— how could he say such a thing when he'd been engaged to a lady doctor? An educated and refined lady, unlike her. "I thought you didn't tell tales, Tom."

He grinned and took one step closer, grasping her right hand with his left. He circled his thumb on her palm, sending tremors through her. Dropping his hand from her face, he wrapped it around her back and pulled her closer, his face inches from hers. She stopped breathing. He was going to kiss her. A man, *this* man, the one she cared for, was going to press his lips to hers. She closed her eyes, ready to feel his mouth caress hers. She sensed the heat of him as his head bent closer. In just one second she'd be kissed.

The door opened behind them and Tom jerked upright. A lamp held aloft cast a cold yellow glow on them. "Oh, it's just you two. Come on in before you catch your death of cold, Jo."

Tom took two steps back. "Mr. Christy, Miss Christy—I wish you both a good evening."

Lying in his bunk, Tom inhaled the wood smoke of the lumberjack's abode. What was the matter with Josephine? Was she angry with her father for his insistence that he would do right by her and marry her? He'd threatened to make sure no schools in Michigan hired him if he left the camp without his daughter. Not that Tom needed to be threatened. What had begun as somewhat of a prank to get the beautiful woman's attention had gotten out of hand. And before he'd known it, he'd fallen head over heels for the fiery cook. But he was also a man of integrity. That day he'd written his mother and asked her for the recipe for her fruitcake and he intended to give it to Jo as a Christmas gift, along with his proposal. He'd have told the truth—she had to make a fruitcake as good as his mother's and she would.

Someone crept toward his bed. The floorboards creaked as Ox sat down on the trunk beside the bunk. "Pa is moving the camp to the Upper Peninsula. We want you to break it to her."

"What?" Tom sat up, leaning on his elbows. "Why don't you do it yourself?"

"She's gonna be roarin' mad when she hears. We figure if you tell her she'll take it better—'specially if you soften it with the offer of marriage."

Tom swallowed hard. This meant he, too, would be moving. "How many of the men already know?"

"None. We're waiting until spring for the move and we'll start telling them after the winter thaw."

"The way we're going, there might not be a hard freeze for a while much less to worry about the thaw."

"You're right. We're a little worried. That's one reason for the decision to move camp soon. Pa bought land and it's been staked."

"What if Jo and I don't want to go with you?"

"Shoot, you can go where you want when the men have gotten their full payment after the winter haul. Just need you to stay and teach the kids till then."

"All right."

"But if you want to come on as teacher up there, Pa'll pay you the same as you'd make as a jack."

The muscles in Tom's shoulders spasmed and he shifted his weight. "Is that what I'll be paid now, too?"

"Only if you take the contract for teacher up there next year."

Jo had said repeatedly that she wanted out of the lumber camps. "So you have me over a barrel."

"Go take a look up there and see what you think before you decide anything. It's mighty pretty."

"Won't be after you log it all out." And he'd helped with that, too. All that White Gold in Michigan pine would be floating down the lake to the mills to be used in America's huge building boom.

Ox patted Tom's shoulder and then rose. "Keep in mind that you have some other men considering on offering my sister marriage. And Pa said if she accepts one of their offers then she won't have to marry you."

Tom snorted. "Jo won't marry anybody she doesn't want to marry, and if she doesn't want me, then I don't want her." Especially after Eugenia's betrayal. He couldn't bear to live through that again.

"We'll see. You think about taking the railroad barge across to check things out." Ox headed to his own bunk.

All Tom could think about, though, were hazel eyes beneath thickly fringed black eyelashes. Reddish-brown hair that curled around an ivory neck. Perfectly coral lips awaiting his kiss. The scent of soft floral combined with flour, sugar, and vanilla. He drifted toward sleep recollecting his arm wrapped around her, the feel of her waist beneath his fingers, the way her lips drew together in contemplation when the camp preacher spoke on the wages of sin, as though this sweet creature had any sins to repent of. Well maybe one, the same as his—stubborn pride. *Lord forgive me for my arrogant attitude and make me worthy of such a fine woman. But if I'm not the one for her, I accept Your will. Amen.*

Reino Talvi slid a piece of paper across the counter toward Jo as the men flowed through the breakfast line. Although he'd been in the country for over twenty years, his mastery of English was still limited. She set down her ladle and opened the note, reading her brother's cramped recording of a Finnish fruitcake recipe. She set it aside.

After passing the lumberjack his breakfast plate, Jo met Mr. Talvi's pale blue eyes, lined by many years that had passed since he'd joined the camps. "So we've had Swedish and French and now we're to try a Finnish variant of fruited cake?"

He rattled off something in Finnish that she didn't understand. Then he patted his shirt pocket, where a five-dollar bill peeked out—which she understood perfectly. *Moose.*

The Finnish man smiled at her. "Bake?" He pointed to the recipe scribbled on a piece of the school children's paper.

She sighed. "Yes, Mr. Talvi, I'll bake."

"Good." He gave her a quick grin but his eyebrows drew together in puzzlement. *Oh no, what if he thought Moose meant it? What if he misunderstood and thought she'd accept a proposal from him?* The man, nearing fifty, was even older than Pa.

Mr. Talvi glanced back at Mrs. Lehto and the widow cocked her head at him.

"You doin' okay, Reino? You look like you seen a ghost."

"No. No ghost. I yoost see pritty lady." He continued to glance in the brunette cook's direction. "You make recipe for Reino?"

Jo exhaled in relief. The Finlander had misunderstood. She'd better warn Mrs. Lehto but the woman was already peering at the recipe.

The line of men continued on. Where was Tom? All night long she'd imagined what his kiss would have felt like. Three men approached the counter together, Tom squeezed between Ox and Moose. *What in the world?*

Ruth passed plates to Ox and Moose but then glanced at Jo. She stepped back and went to the bigger black stove as Jo prepared Tom's plate. She always gave him extra now.

Ox swiped a few biscuits from Tom's plate. "Don't think Tom needs all this additional grub."

"Nope." Moose transferred two sausage links to his plate. "Pretty soon he won't even be taking his breakfast with us."

"Why not?"

Moose and Ox seemed to press in on Tom.

"I'll be resigning my job as axe man soon." He dropped his gaze.

Jo's serving spoon clattered to the floor. "What?" He'd promised. He'd set up this challenge. He'd almost kissed her. Almost. Maybe almost didn't count. No, she wasn't letting him off this easy. If he left, he left with her. But she'd already written a note accepting a job herself. She drew in a slow breath.

"I intend to hold you to your promise."

"Promise?" He raised his dark eyebrows. "Oh, you mean my fruitcake challenge. Yes, ma'am, I plan to keep that wager—but you'll have to produce a cake that meets or exceeds the quality of my mother's." His lips compressed, making them appear thin.

Ma'am? Jo's chin began to twitch. She turned away and untied her apron. Blinking back tears, she headed toward the rear door.

A blaze of black fur brushed against her skirts and then Blue trotted to the door. She pushed through the exit, letting it slam shut. Her breath caught when she spied Pa sitting on the bench, as he whittled a small figure. He'd not taken breakfast with the men this morning but sat outside in the chill. Blue Dog pressed his head against Pa's knee and her father paused to pet him.

"Good boy." He continued to stroke the dog's head as Jo wiped away tears. "I could use some help this morning, Jo—if'n you've got a mind to help your old man."

"Sure, Pa." She sniffed as a headache started at her temple.

"Need some mail to go out. It's on my desk. Can you make sure they take it all—every piece?" He resumed whittling the replica of a tiny Labrador retriever.

Tears streamed down her face. He'd not whittled her a gift for Christmas in over a decade—since she was still a girl. Blue Dog sniffed it, as though he knew the image emerging was of him. Jo wiped away her tears—Ma always said Pa had no stomach for them.

"I'll go over there now if you want." Had he seen her letter to the Bakery in St. Ignace? Was he trying to get her to pull it back before it went out? What a coward she was—she'd not even told him yet.

"Here, Josie." Pa hadn't called her that nickname in years and her tears renewed as he pulled a red handkerchief from his pocket and pressed it into her hand.

"Thanks, Pa."

She bent and kissed his forehead before heading to the office. Inside, a neat stack of letters awaited mailing. Jo sat on her father's high backed oak chair, elaborately carved with acorns, squirrels, and leaves. Pa and Ox had spent many days constructing the beautiful piece.

Jo glanced at the top letter in the stack addressed to Mrs. Horace Jeffries in Tom's even script. Her heartbeat kicked up a notch. Pa's new fountain pen lay atop a pad of paper, inviting her to write down the woman's address. And immediately next to the paper was an envelope. Was this not about the job? Was her father tempting her to write Tom's mother? She drew in a deep breath. A decision had to be made.

God help me.

Before she knew it, Jo had written Mrs. Jeffries a short introductory letter, addressed the envelope, sealed it and handed her missive over with all the others as the postal carrier delivered their mail. She sat in her father's chair for a long while wondering if she'd done the right thing.

But it was too late now.

Chapter 8

Guilt over her decision to send the acceptance letter out on the morrow niggled at Jo all day. The men lingered in the dining hall of the cookhouse, as though too weary to enter back out into the cold and blue-black night. She cast a glance at Tom and was glad he'd not caught her. Somehow she felt he'd know by the look on her face what she had done. She lifted the hinged countertop and entered the kitchen to join her crew as they cleaned up.

"You all right, Jo?" Pearl briskly dried a cast iron skillet and then hung it from a hook overhead.

"Fine." Except she'd snuck and sent a letter to Tom's mother.

"How you findin' time to get ready for Christmas, dear?" Mrs. Peyton stacked the plates.

I need to finish knitting my brothers some new socks. She mentally reviewed every Christmas gift she had begun, but hadn't yet finished. "I haven't."

Ox and Moose stomped up to the counter in their heavy soled boots. Ox jerked a thumb back toward the table where their father was speaking with Tom.

"He says your fruitcake isn't quite as good as his mama's." Ox laughed. "That's a joke."

She wasn't surprised. That exasperating man had called her ma'am, like she was some matron.

Moose leaned in and kissed her cheek. "Of course he's lyin'. Question is—why?"

Did he have a wife back home? A sweetheart? For all she knew, Tom may have a girl in town. But when would he have time since he almost never went to town? Jo nibbled on the inside of her lower lip. It didn't matter. What did count was that by Christmas she'd make Tom admit that she'd prepared a fruitcake even better than his mother's. She'd not backed down from a challenge yet. Why then did this one trouble her so much? Especially after she'd spent time in the Word at night.

Because God wanted her to walk in love—that was the message of Christ's birth.

And now she'd sent the note to Mrs. Jeffries. No taking it back now. But she could pray that God showed her how to turn this mess around. Her hope was ahead of her now—she just needed to get clear on which of the two job offers she preferred. She'd thought it was the bakery. But something, maybe God, made her hesitate today. But once she was sure, then she needed to pack her trunk and have Mr. Brevort drive her into town.

"Thanks, Richard. I mean, *Moose*." How had that scrawny little boy grown up into such a big hairy man?

He patted her cheek then reached into his jacket pocket. "Hey, I have a letter here from a lady looking for work as a camp cook, preferably the manager."

"That's my job." She punched playfully at the thick muscles in his upper arm.

She wasn't ready to tell any of them yet that she intended to accept one of her job offers. But she'd held back the letter of acceptance for the bakery for a few more days. Maybe she'd hear something about the hotel in Newberry, which was a good sixty or more miles from St. Ignace. And farther from her family. An ache began in her chest.

Her youngest brother grinned and held the envelope out of her reach. "Do you want me to show it to Dad?"

She blew out a puff of breath. "Sure."

Ox cocked his dark head at her. "You're not thinking of running off and leaving us, Sis?"

She averted her gaze and spied Tom glancing in her direction. By raising her voice, he should be able to hear her from the front table, where he sat beneath one of the dangling kerosene lamps.

"Why, yes, Moose, I imagine I'll be *married* this Christmas once I've won Mr. Jeffries' fruitcake challenge. So I expect we'll need another cook here. I'm sure as Mrs. Jeffries I'll be living the *high life*."

The men in the front quarter of the room quieted and turned to look toward Jo. From the way her face heated, her cheeks must be as red as the cherries in her muffins. Instead of Tom looking as mortified as she now felt, the aggravating man had the nerve to wink at her and grin.

He stood and snapped his red suspenders. "First you have to win the contest, Miss Christy!"

Scotty McNear called out, "The lass willna marry up with the likes of ye."

His tablemates guffawed and whacked the Scotsman on his back. Someone in the back yelled, "She ain't marryin' no polecat."

Jo laughed.

Mr. Brevort stood. "Josephine wants a mature *homme* like *moi*. But I am already taken." He tugged on his long white beard for emphasis. Low chuckles commenced, followed by a loud sneeze from the Frenchman.

Bandy-legged "Rooster" Rawlings hopped up from his spot next. "Anybody knows I'm the best dancer hereabouts and Jo loves to waltz." He nodded as though agreeing with his own statement. His comrades clapped.

"That's right!" several lumberjacks called out. "And we need some reels and jigs tonight if Tom'll get his fiddle out."

There was so much commotion the lamps began to sway overhead.

Her father rose, stifling the whistles and guffaws. "I never gave my consent for any special purchases to be bakin' different recipes of fruitcake every night till my Jo hits on one that pleases Mr. Jeffries here. So as far as I am concerned, the contest is off."

A collective groan resounded. Jo sank to her stool behind the counter as tears pricked her eyes. Twenty-five years old and yet unmarried. Not that Tom really intended to honor his bet.

About that time Jo heard shouts, rustling, banging, and much conversation echoing up but she couldn't make out the words. Pearl laughed and pulled her apron up to cover her mouth.

Jo sighed. *Only three more weeks till Christmas day.*

Ruth sat down on the floor beside her. "They've taken up another collection to purchase whatever you need to keep baking your recipes, Jo!"

"And the men are going to bring you their mother's recipes."

"Really?"

She nodded. "Christmas and love—goes together perfectly, don't you think?"

Finally the cookhouse was clean for the night. The other ladies had retreated to their cabins to freshen up, in case there was indeed a dance that evening. Although they'd encouraged her to do the same, Jo had wanted to ensure that the kitchen was clean first. She untied her long apron and folded it—no time to wash it tonight. She'd have to do laundry tomorrow morning after the lumberjacks tried out her ginger pancakes. She grinned at the idea of how their faces would contort in surprise when they got a taste of spice in her flapjacks. Maybe this wasn't such a good idea—as soon as they'd gotten a taste of the gingerbread pancakes they'd likely start demanding gingerbread cake for dessert in the evenings. And there was no extra money for cream to go with the treat.

She rubbed her lower back. All alone in the building, she imagined what their Christmas celebration would look like this year. Tears filled her eyes as she thought of Ma not being with them. The door opened then and a gust of wind accompanied Tom Jeffries into the building.

Brushing away tears, she took several steps toward the counter. "What do you need now, Thomas? You got another contest going?" Hopefully one that would put brains back in his head.

He slammed the door behind him and secured the latch. She swallowed as he strode toward her.

"You should unlock that door—what will my brothers think if they try to get in here?"

Tom's cheeks, already pink from outside, reddened further. He twisted his hat in his broad hands. "There's a stiff wind out there—I simply secured the door so it didn't blow open. Besides—your brothers are playing pinochle with the Drake family tonight—said they don't dance."

"What do you want?" She secured her hands on her hips. The closer he came, the harder her heart beat.

"I'll be happy to play the fiddle."

"What?"

"For dancing tonight."

She pressed a hand to her chest in relief. "Oh, yes, that would be wonderful. The folks will enjoy it. Thank you."

He dipped his head slightly. "Was that so hard to say?"

"No, and the ladies will be so happy to return and find you all dancing."

He gazed up at her, eyes flashing. "You're not staying?"

"No, I'm not."

"Don't you like me, Jo?"

She stomped her foot. "When did I ever say I didn't like you, Tom Jeffries?" She glared at him. Problem was she liked him too much. She wasn't about to risk her heart on a lumberjack who was about to light out for parts unknown. So what that he loved all the same books she and Ma had enjoyed together. So what if he loved the camp children as much as she did. So what if being near him twisted her insides into knots and made her want to throw herself into his arms.

"You have a funny way of showing your feelings, Josephine."

Jo scowled at him. He'd be gone soon. "I hear you're planning on leaving your job."

He raised his eyebrows high. "Why, Jo—I thought you knew I had to."

Scotty was right—Tom was a polecat. Jo grabbed her apron, whipped it open and snapped it at him. "Get out of my kitchen."

Backing up, he raised his hands. "See what I mean about your distaste for me." But he laughed. "Mother used to chase me out of her kitchen, too—except ours was a much smaller kitchen house."

"Well, is it any wonder? You have a way of getting under foot."

He grinned and her heart did a strange flip-flop. *Lord have mercy she needed to get this man out of her domain and right quick.* He set his violin case down on the table nearest him.

Moving closer, Tom's direct gaze was filled with longing. She fought the desire to flee yet at the same time she wanted him to pull her into his arms and kiss her like he was about to do when Pa had come out.

"Jo, the men said you love to dance. There's no reason for you to leave just because I'll be here." He cocked his head to the side. "Besides which I'll be playing my fiddle and I won't be able to dance, anyways, so you don't have to be afraid of me asking."

"I'm not afraid of you!"

"Good." He took two steps closer and lifted the hinged countertop to allow himself entry to the kitchen.

After her pronouncement, she couldn't very well back away from him, so Jo stood her ground, a tremor beginning in her knees. She tried to make it stop, to no avail, and now her hands were shaking, too, as Tom took them in his.

"Josephine, I may not have anything to offer you or any other woman..." His thumbs brushed the tops of her trembling hands.

Pa paid the men good wages, better than many. And since he didn't allow carousing, most were able to have a family, if they chose. So what did he mean, by acting poor? Was that going to be one of his excuses for not honoring his challenge? She bit the inside of her lip and averted her gaze.

Tom dropped one hand and gently grasped her chin, turning her face toward his as he leaned closer and whispered in her ear, "Would you care to dance with me now, Miss Christy? In the privacy of your kitchen?"

She was having difficulty breathing, much less making her legs move, but Tom pulled her into his arms, one hand resting on her waist and the other holding her hand high, in position for the waltz. He hummed as he led her in the three steps of the dance, but keeping her in a tight circle so they didn't bump into the stoves and work tables. Every other thought seemed to be swept away, so consumed was she with the feel of his breath on her cheek, his warm hand at her waist, his strong fingers guiding her in the movements. Dizziness threatened to topple her but she drew in slow breaths, feeling his flannel-shirted torso pressed against her, while her heart tried to hammer its way out of her chest to join his. She loved him. She was more certain of it now than she had been before. Then, how could she leave?

One-two-three, around and around they went.

"You're an excellent dancer, Miss Christy." The timbre of his voice and Tom's perfect diction had the effect of chilling her and bringing her to her senses.

He came from a different world than she was from. Both Ox and Moose confirmed that his father was a professor. And his former fiancé was a physician. None of her fruitcakes had pleased him. And none would. Jo stopped moving and pulled back. Tom stumbled and released her.

"What's wrong?" He shoved a hand through his thick hair. "Weren't you enjoying yourself?"

Maybe a little too much. "I'm tired. I'm going home."

"Miss Christy," he said hurriedly, "might I accompany you to the church service again this week?"

She sucked in a breath. "I—well—yes, I'm going." There could be no harm in him going with her to the camp church meeting. Even her brothers couldn't argue with her agreeing to have Tom walk her to church and sitting by her.

Tom grinned. "It's a date, then."

She raised her hands. "No. Going to church is not a date—it is simply worshipping together."

He winked at her. "Whatever you say, Miss Christy."

Jo gritted her teeth.

Banging on the door made her jump. "Jo! Whatya doin' in there?" Ox called out.

"What did I tell you?" Jo heaved a sigh.

He sprinted to the door and threw it open, admitting both brothers.

"Ox?"

Ox pushed past and Tom headed toward Jo. "He botherin' you?"

She was tempted to snap her brother with the apron, too. "Of course he is—I swear he's worse than you two are!"

"Came to walk you home—the wind's picked up out here."

"Thank you, Ox. Mr. Jeffries failed to offer to see me to the cabin safely. No doubt hoping flying debris would knock me senseless so I'd forget his wager."

Ox laughed and faced Tom. "No chance of her forgettin'—you did it in front of her Angel crew."

"Her Angel crew?"

"The camp cooks. She'd never live it down if she didn't make the best fruitcake ever—you wait and see!" Ox threw his head back and guffawed.

Heat flowed up her neck and Jo shook her head. "Garrett, you're not helping things."

Chapter 9

Fifteen days till Christmas.

Daylight and the rooster crowing woke Jo just as she dreamed about adding Cardamom to a fruitcake recipe. The one spice she didn't have yet. In her dream, Ma was right there with her, helping. She rubbed her eyes and looked around the cabin. Pa was already gone to get the fires going in the stove, so she rushed through her morning ablutions.

As head cook, and with more help, Jo had been able to delegate the prep work to the other ladies. She opened the door to the cookhouse but spied neither hide nor hair of her assistants. But everything was laid out in readiness for breakfast.

"Pa?"

"Yup?" his voice rose from behind the counter, where he was bent over the stove.

"Where is everybody?"

"Don't know." He stood. "But you tell them I'll dock their pay if they make it a habit."

"I can see they set everything up, though."

"Mighty peculiar." Pa shrugged. "And Jo—if you need help, I have another lady very interested in starting right after Christmas."

She nodded as she moved forward to join her father in the kitchen. Someone's new starter ingredients, for yet another fruitcake recipe, filled a large bowl.

"Might make your life a little easier if someone else hired on for the kitchen." Pa quirked an eyebrow at her.

Jo bit her tongue. She'd still not sent her letter to the bakery. Swiftly cracking three eggs, she added them to the bowl and then poured in the cup of cream someone had left alongside a faded recipe on which was scrawled, "Aunt Jean's Christmas muffins."

The back door opened and Blue Dog trotted in with Ox. "The ladies all went out to talk to the peddler."

Pa scowled. "Told that man to get permission from me before he came into my camp, again."

"Aw, it's old Mr. Perry. He's harmless. And he's got some nice toys the kids will like." Ox patted his jacket pocket. "And some good candy, too."

Their father narrowed his eyes. "Still gonna go have a little chat with him and gather those gals back in where they belong."

Jo shook her head. "Give them a minute, Pa. They've been working so hard."

He moved closer to her, eyeing the fruitcake muffin batter. "All right."

Pa must be missing Ma as much as she was because he didn't give her any argument. She whisked the contents in the bowl together, forming a thick batter. She grabbed a pan of melted butter and added the contents. Then she poured the mixture into the muffin tins that had been arranged along the counter. Whoever was trying out this recipe apparently planned on only making two dozen muffins, which meant not all of the men would receive one. That wasn't going to work. They'd have to make more.

"A letter came from Tom's mother." Her brother waved the missive in front of her face then held it out of reach.

"Give it to me."

"Not unless you let me have the batter bowl."

"Is that all?" She shoved the remainder across the counter to him and he dipped his fingers along the sides.

"Save some for me, son." Pa grabbed a spatula and scooped up a mouthful, then licked his lips. "Tastes pretty close to your Ma's recipe."

Tears pricked Jo's eyes. She'd never taste Ma's good cooking again. She turned from her father and brother to examine her letters, and sniffed.

Right behind Mrs. Jeffries's letter was one from The Tahquamenon Inn, in Newberry, a growing town in Michigan's Upper Peninsula. Jo slid the missive into her apron packet, collapsed down onto her low stool, ripped open Mrs. Jeffries' letter.

Dear Miss Christy,

I am so delighted that my Thomas is attending camp church service with you and your family. He was always a boy of strong faith, at least until his sister died. And I'm glad to hear you've found him reading his Bible, too. I'm sorry he doesn't get a chance to ride much—he so loved his horse, when he was growing up. I am arranging to get the books he wants to him by Christmas. And bless you for encouraging him to tutor the children from the camp school. I'm sure Thomas told you all about his desire to teach, but with our great country's difficult economic times, he felt he could support me better by obtaining work. Of course, very soon he will no longer need to send money home as I will no longer be here. I shall be gone before much longer. Please keep me in your prayers.

Many Blessings, Cordelia Jeffries

Tom had wanted to be a teacher—that didn't seem like a big surprise. Too bad that he'd not been able to pursue his dreams. But she'd been trapped, too. Jo re-read Mrs. Jeffries' last lines. Why would the woman no longer be there?

Pa eyed something on the floor and reached down to snatch it up. The letter from the business in Newberry. She stiffened as he glanced at the letter.

Pa handed her the envelope. "This is for you, Jo."

Embarrassed, she averted her gaze. She should have spoken with her father by now.

"Daughter?"

She looked up as her brother set aside the bowl and departed, Blue Dog trailing him.

"Yes, Pa?"

"This Tom is a good man."

She nodded slowly, flabbergasted at his words.

He poked the letter from the inn. "Do you know what you are doing, darlin' girl?"

Yes. She was going to have a life. She was getting out of the lumber camps and never coming back. But tears pricked her eyes. "No, Pa, I don't think I do."

Vanilla, sugar, and flour scented air saturated the building, teasing Tom's senses. The promise of sugar cookies distracted the children from his reading of Mark Twain's Huckleberry Finn.

Jo approached their table, clutching a basket filled with muslin bags. He couldn't help staring at the beautiful woman who'd drawn him as no other. What had he been thinking when he'd proposed to

Eugenia? They'd been childhood friends, were compatible, and he'd been willing to wait for her to finish school. But when she'd gotten a better offer, he was discarded. Even now, his stomach clenched at the memory. Would Jo Christy reject him, too?

All twelve of his primer-level pupils glanced up from the table where they sat, piles of evergreens covering the surface.

"Miss Jo!" Mandy called out and ran to give her a hug.

"Careful—you'll crush the cookies."

"Thanks Miss Christy!" Each child took a small cloth bag filled with sugar cookies.

"There's a jar of frosting in the bottom of each bag so don't go swinging them around." Jo opened one, to demonstrate.

The white icing Jo made for desserts reminded him of the snowdrifts he'd expected to find up North. He glanced out the window where light snow drifted down. With the mild winter they'd had so far, the old-timers claimed there was no danger that they could be snowed in anytime soon.

"I have a sack for you, too, Mr. Jeffries." A soft smile tugged at her lovely lips as she passed the bag to him, gently setting it down on the table.

"Thank you. You're very kind."

As appealing as the treats were, he desired to feast his eyes on her more than he wished to receive cookies. Perhaps she'd sit down for a minute.

"Miss Jo, we all brought holly branches to decorate the tables with." Mandy held up the berry-covered limb to demonstrate.

"Why, that's lovely." Her eyes widened. "Why don't you put some on every table while I talk with <u>Mr.</u> Jeffries?"

His anticipation fled at her cool tone of voice.

The children looked to him and he gave a quick nod of assent. The laughed and rose, carrying away the spicy scent of the holly.

"Tom?"

He looked up into her hazel eyes, her reddish-brown eyebrows bunching together.

She placed a gentle hand on his shoulder. "Is your … do you have any reason to believe your mother might be ill?"

Her touch invited him to cover her hand with his, but he resisted the impulse.

"No. She's not said a thing in her letters to me." If anything, his mother sounded feistier than ever. He frowned.

Jo's pretty lips bunched up. "I think you should ask her."

"Why would you say such a thing … unless …" Anger rose up in him.

The telling stain of apple red splotches on her cheeks revealed her secret. "Tom…"

"You've been corresponding with my mother, haven't you?"

He shoved back from the table. With another man, he wasn't averse to using his height to intimidate, but now, with this slight woman, he felt like a coward and collapsed back into his chair. Unfair tactics went against his personal code of ethics.

Several of the children turned in their direction and he motioned for them to turn back around.

Jo stopped chewing on her lower lip. "Yes, I have."

"That's cheating." He fisted his hands. If he hated anything it was dishonesty. Worse, though, was a bully. He forced himself to relax.

"No, it isn't—you never said I couldn't." She lifted her chin.

Smart little minx. Some of his ire evaporated. "So did she give you the recipe?"

Jo huffed. "Tom, I'm more concerned about your mother than your silly contest."

His stomach clenched. He rose again. "I'll get a telegram out to her if you think I should."

Her now pale face answered his question. But why would Mother tell Jo, a stranger, and not him? Was this all just a game to Jo, like it had started with him? Was she so determined to humiliate him by rejecting him, as some of the shanty boys suggested, that she'd weasel her way into his mother's good graces and get the recipe? He'd prayed and this may be God's answer. He took a deep breath.

"Miss Christy, I want to apologize for behaving in such a disrespectful manner toward you."

Her eyebrows bunched together, but she didn't respond.

"I never should have made that offer to you. It isn't the proper way for two people to even consider marrying one another."

"Stop. That's enough." She held up a hand. Tears glistened in her eyes and he felt like a cad.

"Please …" He wanted to explain that he'd been wrong. To apologize. To make it right.

She tossed a bag of cookies at him, narrowly missing his nose. Then she fled the building.

Oh, Lord, I've only made things worse.

If that wasn't a sign from God, Jo didn't know what it was. Her stomach threatened to empty its contents as she marched to the office, went inside, and pulled her acceptance letter from the drawer. Sitting in Pa's chair, she let her tears drip down onto her apron. How had she been such a fool? Tom had led her to believe he had feelings for her—he'd almost kissed her, for heaven's sake. He'd danced with her. She sure wasn't going to sit there and listen to any more of his excuses why he wanted to renege on his challenge. Sniffing, she ran her finger over the bakery's address. Then she went in search of Frenchie. She didn't want to wait until the mail wagon arrived.

No wonder none of the German, French, and British versions of fruited Christmas cake had met his approval—he'd never intended to marry her. At least now she could stop, for she'd finally lost her enthusiasm for the battle. After all, Christmas was about the love of Christ and his birth and not about silly contests. She'd won the biggest gift of all the day she'd given her life over to the Lord. And lately, she'd not been acting like it. She had two secure job offers in the Upper Peninsula, a God who loved her, and a life that would be just fine without Tom Jeffries.

Jo located Frenchie in the livery stable, cleaning bridles.

"Why so sad, *ma petite*?" He wiped his hands and set aside his rag.

"I need to get this out in the mail, but I didn't send it when he delivered earlier in the week."

"And you want old Frenchie to take it?"

She needed to go, too, to purchase new clothing for the job. She'd need to purchase readymade frocks, having no time to sew. "I need to go to town, too."

The ache that filled her chest felt almost as bad as the loss she experienced when Ma had died.

"Has that rascal done something to hurt you, *ma chère?*"

"No." She accepted the handkerchief he handed her and blew her nose. Her own stupidity had brought this upset about. Believing Tom really had begun to care for her. Thinking that he might be the one for her. Continuing in efforts that had been met with rejection over and over again.

"Perhaps you are grieving your *maman, n'est pas?*"

"Yes." This ache was like having a wound ripped open that had just begun to heal. If only Ma had given her the money she'd intended to leave her, before she'd died. Who knew what Pa had done with the dollars she'd saved for her over the years. At least thinking about that made her feel less guilty about what she was about to do.

"Tomorrow I will bring you to town, first thing. *Bien?*"

"Yes, that's good. Thank you."

From there, Jo sought out Irma and the older woman agreed to substitute for the evening meal. Jo spent the early evening going through her drawers and sorting out what she'd need to take with her when she moved to St. Ignace. Something inside her withered like the leaves that had all drifted down to the ground.

A blessed numbness sealed her sleep, like it had the weeks after Ma's death. She slept deeper than she had in ages.

A sharp rap at her window awoke Jo and she sat straight up in bed, throwing off her quilts. She'd not even heard Pa leave that morning. She went to the window and peered out at Frenchie.

"*Allons.* Come on." He pulled his red knit hat lower on his head.

She held up five fingers. "Five minutes."

"*Oui.*"

As quickly as she could, she donned her clothes and coat, hat, and gloves and headed out. The trip to town was uneventful, save for the deer that jumped in front of them. Once in town, Jo clutched her reticule to her breast and headed to the docks to learn what the current cost of a ticket across would be. Although the increase in price was slight, it meant she'd have to do without new undergarments until she received her first paycheck. Reworking her list, she crossed the street, dodging carriages and drays as well as horse manure.

Frenchie emerged from the post office. "*C'est fini*—it's done."

Was she making a huge mistake? The sadness overcoming her screamed that she had no other choices. "Thank you."

"Here—for you." The Frenchman handed a missive to her.

Another one, already, from Mrs. Jeffries.

"You want to go in where it is warm—to read?"

"Yes. Go ahead to the mercantile and I'll catch up with you in a bit." Jo ducked back into the post office. She settled on a bench near the door and tore open the envelope. She pulled the single sheet of rosewater-scented paper free and held the note up by the nearby window.

Dear Josephine,

If it is within your power, I'd greatly appreciate it if you encourage Thomas to remain in camp over the holidays. It would be in his best interests to do so. I am in the process of putting my affairs in order and it would be futile for him to try to visit me at this time. Has Thomas mentioned anything from home that he wishes he had with him there? I would hate to depart from here without him having received anything he desired from the old homestead. I don't know how much longer I'll be on this earth. Please keep this letter private between the two of us.

Blessings and prayers to you, my dear. Cordelia

Jo sucked in a deep breath. If Tom's mother had grown seriously ill and Tom wanted the special fruitcakes she makes, then what would happen if she died? By golly, she had to ask Mrs. Jeffries straight out for the recipe. Jo would get it for him, in honor of his mother, and not for herself. Suddenly, a load seemed lifted from her.

She approached the counter. "May I purchase a sheet of paper and an envelope? And may I borrow your fountain pen?"

No other patrons were present but the man behind the counter peered around as though searching someone out. "Here." He shoved a notepad at her and his pen.

"Much obliged, sir."

"Don't tell anyone."

"I won't." She scribbled her request.

85

"Envelope?"

When she nodded, he slid one across the counter. She hastily addressed the letter and then paid for postage.

She frowned. Her intent was to run away from Tom, not get close to him and encourage him to stay at camp. Maybe she should tell him what his mother said. *No.* She'd honor the woman's request.

Stepping out into the cold air, Jo's head began to pound, like the sound of the horse's hooves clamoring over the cobblestone streets. She practically ran to the store so she wouldn't freeze in the cold. A gentleman in a tall beaver hat held the door open for her as she stepped into the warmth of the mercantile.

"Awfully cold, isn't it, Miss?" The man removed his hat and tucked it under his arm.

Shivering, she bobbed her chin in agreement.

"Why Lawyer Cain, what brings you here?" The portly owner grasped the attorney's hand.

Jo went about her business, filling her basket with the few things she could afford and that she needed for her new job. She could almost smell the multitudes of scents that the bakery in the Upper Peninsula would have. But maybe that was because she was standing beside the spice section. A tiny glass jar of cardamom seemed to call her name. She lifted it from the display and discretely removed the cover. Inhaling deeply, her heart first rose, thinking this might be exactly what she needed for the fruitcake. Then just as quickly her spirits crashed. Tom had already made it clear he was very sorry for what he'd said. Still, she needed it in case it was required in his mother's recipe. Surely the woman would send her the directions before Christmas has arrived.

"On sale today, Miss Christy." The clerk grinned and gave her the new price.

She might have just enough to cover it.

Frenchie joined her and swiped the bottle from her hands. "With my order, *oui*?"

"Yes. Thank you."

As soon as Frenchie's purchases for the camp were tallied, he and the shop owner began loading them into the dray.

Jo left with everything she needed—except her composure. Because as she departed with her goods, the clerk asked her, "Say, when's the wedding date for you and your young man?"

When she'd stared gape-mouthed at him, he'd continued, "The one who bought those nice boots for you."

Swallowing hard, she'd gathered up her purchases. "I fear the poor man didn't have my pa's permission and I was unaware of that particular shanty boy's doings until recently. He's gonna be mighty disappointed when he discovers I've taken work in St. Ignace."

Her cheeks burned for she shouldn't have blurted out these comments to the salesclerk. But she was so embarrassed and angry that her tongue had come unhinged. She ducked her head.

Would Tom be *relieved* rather than disappointed?

Chapter Ten

In for a penny, in for a silver dollar.

Although Tom fully expected Jo to return from town and scorn him, instead she acted as though she was right as rain. Watching her finish serving, he observed again that her attempts for him to be happy with her baking efforts weren't nearly as desperate as before. A calm had settled over her. Her father, on the other hand, turned agitated and now made almost daily trips to Mackinaw City, sometimes not returning until the following night.

As he watched Sven inhaling a piece of a fruited Italian coffee cake, Tom had no desire to take even one bite. Truth be told, he was plum full up on fruitcake. He wasn't even sure he'd recognize his own mother's recipe if she baked it herself, he'd consumed so many variants.

Jo slid in next to him, bringing the scent of lilac water and the rum flavoring of the coffee cake. She smiled, and her peaceful expression touched his heart. She really seemed to have forgiven him for his ridiculous act of arrogance. Maybe they could start over.

He couldn't forget the feel of her in his arms, as they'd danced.

"Tom, don't worry about even trying this one tonight. We made it for Leonardo Zandi." She waved at the new axe man, a handsome Italian. Was he the reason Jo practically glowed?

The cheeky fellow stood, kissed his fingertips, and then opened his arms toward Jo. She blushed and returned her attention to Tom.

He stabbed his fork into his pork roast, then slowly sliced himself a chunk and brought it to his lips.

Jo cocked her head in what in any other woman would be a coquettish manner. "I'm hoping you'll help me plan the Christmas pageant tonight."

He'd been considering taking the train home to Ohio for a week or so, at least until he figured out what was transpiring with his mother.

"We really need you, Tom." Jo leaned in, her voice low, almost husky. The room suddenly seemed too small and too hot, but they were seated well away from the pot-bellied stove that heated the room, along with the stoves up front.

Two tiny hands suddenly covered his eyes. He returned his fork to his plate.

"We need you to play your fiddle and read some stories for our Christmas pageant." Mandy's stilted pronouncement sounded as though she'd been coached.

He pulled her fingers away. "Why should I?"

"'Cause Miss Jo wants you there. I think she loves you." The little girl drew the "loves" out long and loud, resulting in the other lumberjacks hearing and laughing.

But instead of acting offended, Jo beamed beatifically. Could it be? Had she fallen for him as he had for her? He flexed his shoulders. Len Zandi wasn't about to usurp his rights. The man was new. Maybe he didn't know about the fruitcake challenge. Tom's heart pounded with such strength he could hear it in his ears, over the cacophony of the cook shack's noise. Would Zandi stand and offer for Jo?

Tom placed his arm around Jo as little Mandy ducked beneath, his arm now covering both hers and Jo's shoulders. "What are you doing in here tonight, anyways, my star pupil?"

"Just wanted to make sure you got the message."

"Oh, I've got it all right." He hoped he did. He gazed into Jo's eyes. "I'll be here for Christmas."

Jo's shoulders slumped and she leaned her head back, stretching her neck. "I'm glad."

She was happy about him staying. Warmth spread through his chest.

With a giggle, Mandy ducked back out from under his arm and skipped off between the rows of jacks.

He squeezed his sweetheart's shoulder. "We got off to a rocky start, but I want to do right by you, Jo."

She stiffened, but he left his arm around her, even when her brother gave him the evil eye from his spot.

"I have forgiven you for what you got started. And we've had a lot of fun." Jo's smile looked forced. "The men have enjoyed all the desserts. And it sure has distracted me from thinking about my Ma."

When tears appeared in her eyes, he pulled out his clean monogrammed handkerchief and handed it to her.

They ate the rest of their dinner in companionable silence and then Tom helped them clean up, singing some Christmas carols with the ladies. Jo appeared more animated than ever. Happy. He loved seeing her enjoying the joy of the season. The future didn't seem grim at all, if she were in it.

But could he support her? He had to know what kind of life he'd be offering her in the Upper Peninsula. She'd not wanted to remain in a lumber camp, but that was the only teaching offer he had—from her father.

Mr. Christy had him over a barrel.

"Goodnight." Pearl waved goodbye as she and Frenchie left the building.

Just Jo and Tom remained, alone. Suddenly nervous, she held perfectly still as he wrapped her new fur-lined cape around her, a gift an Odawa woman she and mother had helped when her husband, a trapper, had died. The pretty woman remarried quickly and brought the gift and her new baby and husband by the camp right after she'd returned from town.

But was it the warmth of the fur that felt so comforting or the gentleness of Tom's hands as he rearranged her hair inside of the hood?

"I'm glad you understand about my error and are willing to give me another chance, Jo."

He took two steps closer and grasped her hands in his, sending a tingle up her arms. "There are some things I have to figure out for myself before I can make any plans that include a wife."

She stifled the urge to snort in laughter. He'd be figuring out those things all by his lonesome because she had no intention of being there. As for plans—she had her own. She chewed on her lower lip, wondering why the bakery hadn't responded to her letter. They were supposed to give her a definite date to start her position.

Still, she couldn't help but look at his handsome face and wonder what it would have been like to look at him every day for the rest of their lives. Growing old together. But such was not to be.

"Don't look so worried, Jo. I know God has a plan for both of us."

His eyes, so large and luminous, drew her attention.

"Yes, He does."

She shouldn't be thinking about kissing him. She *should* be telling him all about her suspicions about his mother, so he could go see her.

"You seem so preoccupied tonight." Tom ran two fingers alongside her jaw and she held her breath.

She slowly exhaled as he removed his hand from alongside her face, feeling suddenly sad at the loss of contact.

He leaned in toward her. "Jo?"

She had to keep him here—that had to be the reason she was rising up on her tiptoes as his head bent closer.

"Yes." Closing her eyes, Jo waited for his kiss, her heart hammering in her chest.

Tom wrapped his arms around her and drew her against him. Her face brushed the heavy wool of his jacket. She drew in a breath. She shouldn't lead him on. She didn't…

His warm lips covered hers and the sweetness of the kiss made her cling to him. He groaned as he released her but then kissed her again, with more fervor than the first kiss, his mouth covering hers with firm pressure. Oh, if this kiss would never end. If only she could have this experience every day for the rest of her life. She leaned further into him.

Tom pulled away, and bent to lean his forehead against hers. "Jo, oh my sweet Josephine."

A sudden 'thwack' of a branch blown into the exterior wall caused Jo to jump. Then they both laughed. He pulled her into his embrace and rested his chin on top of her head.

"I don't know what we're going to do, sweetheart, but promise me you'll be patient with me."

How could she promise that? She'd already accepted the job in St. Ignace. But he'd called her his sweetheart. Instead of saying anything, she tipped back her head and offered her lips.

He laughed. "Only one more. I don't want to lose what control I have left."

This kiss was gentle, like rose petals brushing her lips. They tingled and she wanted more. But he kept his word and released her.

Tom turned her her toward the door. "Off we go, my angel."

His angel. She was no angel. And soon, off she would be going—away from him, the camp, and her family.

"All aboard." The railroad worker gestured Tom toward the dock, where the train awaited transportation across the straits.

They'd be pulled by steam tugboat across the wide expanse where Lakes Michigan and Lake Huron met. At least the brilliant sapphire water was fairly calm today.

As he moved forward, several nuns wearing habits covered by thick capes, accompanied him. The priest with the group smiled at Tom. "What brings you across the water, young man?"

"Going to the Upper Peninsula to check out a new lumber camp."

"Plenty of those going up, that's for sure." The man's small build would never have suited him as a shanty boy—unless perhaps he was a limber.

The nuns turned to him and nodded. They waited for the priest to join them before they boarded. The boat horn tooted loudly and the small group startled.

Behind Tom, he sensed someone watching him, but when he turned, he only saw a woman with a young boy, two large men dressed in black overcoats and beaver hats, and a woman bent slightly forward, covered in a shabby tan coat, a moth-eaten shawl wrapped over her head, and well-worn deerskin gloves covering her hands. Odd, the sensation that he knew her, but with her head bent down against the wind, he couldn't tell if he'd run across the woman in town before.

What a strange sensation for Jo to board only a section of train that had been separated from its engine. The back section was loaded with Christmas goods ordered for residents of St. Ignace and parts further east in the Upper Peninsula. The car would be reattached to an engine once they arrived on the mainland. Jo kept her head down as she inched past Tom, who seemed engaged in conversation with several nuns. They laughed as she passed them to take her seat in the back.

What was he doing here on this same railroad train, being pulled on a barge across the straits? Pa had left that morning to visit Ma's sister in Traverse City, promising to bring her mother's fruitcake recipe back. Jo hadn't had the heart to tell him it didn't matter.

What if Tom had taken advantage of Pa's absence to depart the camp, never to return? Her cheeks heated in anger. He'd promised to help with the Christmas show; the children had worked so hard, practicing all their favorite carols. She could already feel their disappointment.

It didn't matter. She was leaving, too, and that would also upset them. Still, his behavior only reinforced that she lacked discernment in matters of the heart. She had allowed him to kiss her. And she wanted him to kiss her more. All the while knowing that he regretted making his challenge. She pulled his monogrammed handkerchief from her pocket and fingered the raised white silk thread forming a "J" on the soft linen cloth.

Regardless of anything Tom chose to do, she would be fine. God promised her in His Word. As the tugboat pulled away from the dock, pulling the barged train behind it, Jo hummed Christmas carols to herself, trying to distract herself from thinking what might happen if they were to sink into the icy water.

Ahead of her, Tom leaned his head toward the glass, apparently napping. How could he sleep while rocking along like this? She took the opportunity to move up several seats. With rapt attention, she gazed out at Mackinac Island, as they passed by. So many newcomers had settled there. And although she'd looked into a job on the island, most positions were seasonal.

After a while, Tom shook his head and sat up, then turned to look at the priest, across the aisle from him.

"Do you have the time?"

The clergyman pulled out a brass watch, secured with a chain to his pocket. "Almost ten."

"We should be there soon, I hope."

"Yes, we have a lunch to attend at St. Anne's today. Where do you need to be?"

Tom shrugged. "I'm a teacher. I'm going to check on my school site."

Acid filled Jo's gut. He was a teacher already? Was he trained then? Why had he never said? Or was he lying like Arnault had? So he'd already secured his position and was, indeed leaving. She groaned. What if he was working in St. Ignace, right where she'd be? She'd never live down the humiliation if people discovered what had happened.

Keeping her head down, Jo prayed and rested her eyes for a while. When she looked up again, she spied the shoreline of St. Ignace, and the dark outline of the railroad dock, where the tugboat was headed with them.

"Are you married, son?" The priest's voice carried back to her tingling ears.

"No, Father." Was it her imagination or did Tom sound regretful?

Jo jumped when the tugboat sounded a greeting to another as it maneuvered the barge into the dock. She retrieved a mint lozenge from the tin in her reticule.

"Where's your school situated?" One of the nuns asked Tom.

Popping the candy into her mouth, Jo savored its sweet spearmint flavor.

"About ten miles out of town—at the new Christy Camp."

Jo almost gagged. She spit the lozenge out before she choked on it. Pa had already purchased yet one more camp for them to move to? He'd promised he'd tell her well in advance of any change. Just like he'd done with Ma, he'd probably not tell Jo until the week before they had to pack up and leave. So inconsiderate of others when he had his mind fixed on something.

But if Tom was going out to the camp, and he was going to teach, then he was in on it too. Yet another man seeking to control her. At least he might not be trying to escape her.

Men shouted from the docks as the barge was positioned to have the railroad car detached. The car rocked as the tug released it. Suddenly dizzy, Jo bent her head and remained seated, even though the others were gathering up their belongings to depart.

"Railroad dock, St. Ignace!" the conductor called out.

Jo waited for Tom to leave the car, nauseated more from her father's secret than the rolling sensation from crossing the straits.

All she had to do now was get to the bakery and find out when her new life would start.

As Tom exited, the conductor pressed a piece of tobacco into his cheek. "Home now for me."

"You live here?"

"For now, but once those new rail line run out to the lumber camps east of here I might try to get a little cabin closer to my son. He's logging near the Tahquamenon River."

"So the train will bring people out to the camps?"

"All those lines, whether for hauling logs or people, will soon crisscross the entire Upper Peninsula. Railroad towns were springing up right and left."

"You don't say." Probably why Mr. Christy was anxious to move the camp.

Tom watched out of the corner of his eye, as the shabbily dressed passenger in the back remained seated. Why hadn't that poor women disembarked?

The conductor followed his gaze. "Guess I'll have to urge her to leave the train, eh?"

Tom walked quickly up the dock, catching up with the Catholic priest and nuns. "If I don't see you again, I'd like to wish you a wonderful Christmas."

The nuns smiled and the priest's eyes sparkled. "You as well, young man. I have a feeling God has many blessings ahead for you."

The comment warmed Tom's heart yet something else tugged at him to try to help the lady from the back of the train. Ducking behind a large square column on the railroad dock platform supporting the overhang, Tom waited until the woman passed.

As she did, he glimpsed her profile. *Jo.* His heart stuck in his throat. Maybe her brothers had told the truth the other night—she was intending to leave the camps for good. Either that or she was there to check out the new camp, as Ox and Moose had already done, declaring it "full of the best hardwoods we've seen yet." But surely her brothers would have mentioned that to him, because they knew where he was headed today and they said nothing about their sister.

With Jo now a good twenty feet ahead, Tom ducked out from behind the pillar and followed her. He needed to get to the livery to take a rental horse out to the camp.

The air on this side of the water seemed more stagnant. The buildings clustered near the main street were older and there was a stronger Chippewa influence than in Mackinaw City. Log cabin businesses were commonplace as were ancient-looking buildings hewn from stone. The people walking on the board sidewalk all greeted Jo, and then him, as he followed her. A friendly bunch of strangers. Bells jingled when doors were opened, and on the horses that pulled carriages down the sleet-covered street. When he passed a small cedar-sided church building, the strains of "O Holy Night" carried out.

Soon, he'd celebrate his first Christmas with Jo. He prayed it would be the first of many to come.

Jo hadn't dressed properly to go into the bakery. For some crazy reason, today she'd wanted to wear Ma's old clothes and smell the scent of her that remained in their fibers. She'd first check on the shop and then go change inside one of the large outhouses behind the businesses. She'd just hold her breath when she did so. She hesitated, by a fire pot full of burning wood - turning to coals, and warmed her hands. Then she continued in the frigid air that worked its way through her clothing with every step. Soon she was on LaMotte Street.

No shadow of a sign darkened the corner of the storefront windows as she neared the white building. Her breath hitched. But with several steps more she spied something hanging from the door.

She exhaled in relief. With five quick strides she sidestepped the people on the boardwalk, smiling at each as she did so. She clutched her coat closed at her throat and tugged her scarf up over her chin, then came to an abrupt stop.

CLOSED, the placard proclaimed in dark red block letters. Jo lifted her skirts as she stepped over a puddle of slush on the steps that led to the establishment. No welcoming lights glowed inside. She leaned far to the left, glancing through the mullioned windows. Squinting to better see inside the dark interior, her eyes discerned nothing but an empty shop. No tables and chairs. No whitewashed counters that separated the customers from the bakery staff. The cast iron stoves sat cold, alone. Nothing left of her dream. She looked more closely at the sign. Beneath CLOSED was written "Until Further Notice."

Passersby gazed quizzically at her as she lingered, unable to believe the business had closed. She retraced her steps, in a fog, unable to believe what she'd just seen. Why was God punishing her? Her Pa was moving them. Tom was planning to stay in camp, but as a teacher. No one was communicating their plans with her.

Have you? The words were almost audible and Jo glanced around.

Then she saw him. Tom shoved his hands into his pockets and marched toward her, closing the distance.

When he drew her into his arms, Jo knew she had found home. Maybe she'd still be working in the lumber camp. Maybe she'd even have to keep cooking. But if they were together, she'd be at home.

"I'm sorry, Jo." He kissed her forehead. "Your brothers told me you wanted out of the camp and you told me yourself."

She nodded against his chest.

"And I'm perceiving that the bakery was where you'd hoped to start your new life."

"Yes."

"I'll do everything within my power to help you find where you need to be, Jo. Even if that means you're far away from me."

She sniffed and then pulled back to look up at him. "You're going to take a job as teacher in Pa's new camp."

"Don't know yet." He kissed her cheek. "Come on."

"Where are we going?"

"Back to the railroad dock."

"Okay."

"No argument?"

"No."

He took her hand and they hurried through the blowing wet snow toward the dock.

Chapter Eleven

Cordelia Jeffries handed the train conductor her ticket before climbing aboard and selecting a seat by the window. The last leg of her journey. Her trunks had been placed on the baggage car. All that was left of her old life. She'd left Ohio soil for good. The thought pricked her conscience—perhaps she shouldn't have written her letters to Miss Christy in a language that intimated her demise was swiftly arriving. She laid her carpetbag on the floor by her feet then reached in to pull out four letters to re-read by the sunlight streaming through the window. After she set the missives on her lap, she arranged her wool skirts around the bag.

The train compartment rapidly filled, as others moved through to find an open space. Train travel had made travel so much easier than the old days. A family of four, the mother clutching her child's hand, passed by. Cordelia smiled, remembering how Tom had to be held by both her and Hiram to keep him from running. Her grin wilted—her daughter, Emily, was left behind in Ohio, buried in her lifelong church's cemetery.

Leaning back against the overstuffed leather seat, Cordelia opened the first letter, typed on crisp white paper. Once again she read Mr. Skidmore's words—she was, indeed, the proud owner of her own restaurant, the Grand Northern. A real bona fide businesswoman. Times were changing across this vast country and now she was part of it. She slid the letter back into its official-looking envelope and shuffled it to the bottom of the pile.

Next she opened Mr. Christy's letter of introduction. He must love his daughter very much to wish her to be happy. Written on a plain piece of ledger paper, his writing scrawled across the page, speaking to her as one parent to another. She folded it back up before reading Josephine's final letter to her, before Cordelia had sold the farm and packed up her belongings. The girl had gumption and she'd need it with Tom as her husband. Bless her heart, Josephine finally, after some finagling, asked straight out for the recipe. Cordelia laughed as she folded the floral notepaper and slipped it into its matching envelope.

"Anyone sitting here, ma'am?" A handsome man, about her age, dressed in the heavy wool pants and red and black checked wool coat glanced toward the back and Cordelia followed his gaze. All the other seats were taken.

"No. Have a seat, sir."

He smelled of wood smoke and pine—nothing like Hiram, who favored bay rum and plenty of it. "Thank you."

The man looked like a lumberjack, with broad shoulders that spilled over into her space. Cordelia slid a little closer to the window.

"Sorry if I'm crowding you, ma'am." He tried to scrunch himself, but the effort failed.

She laughed. "It's all right. I'm used to it. My husband, rest his soul, was a big man and so is my son." Cordelia gazed into his coffee-colored eyes.

The man laughed. "My two boys are even bigger than me—I think they'd make them each pay for two seats if they got on the train."

"Oh my." Cordelia fingered the last letter in her lap. She wanted to linger on Tom's words again.

"I wouldn't be on this train if it wasn't for my daughter." He frowned. "And if it wasn't for my wife having passed away."

"I'm so sorry."

The man's eyes misted but he drew in a long breath as though steadying himself. "You have children, so you understand how it can be—you want them to be happy."

"Indeed—that's why I've made this long trip from Ohio." Part of the reason, anyway.

"Ohio? Why, ma'am, you're fortunate we've got such a mild winter this year or you'd not be traveling down these tracks. At least not with such ease."

"I'm so grateful weather has permitted me to come this far. I'd heard about the change in climate this year when I made my plans."

"Not so good for logging but good for travelers." He patted his legs and offered a warm smile. "What brings you so far north?"

"I'm bringing a gift for my son."

"He'll be mighty pleased, I'd bet." The man tilted his head toward her, and she could more readily see what fine features he had. "I just took this train up and back to the next town today to get my daughter something—kind of a gift, too. Though with all the money I've been shellin' out in the past month for her baking efforts, I'm losing hope of this young fella, makin' a half-hearted effort to woo her, is gonna do the right thing by my Josephine."

"Oh!" Cordelia's hands trembled and dislodged Tom's letter from her lap.

The note slid onto the man's knee and he clapped a broad hand down over it. He picked Tom's note up and handed it to Cordelia but as she tried to take it, he held it fast.

"Cordelia Jeffries? That you? And this letter is from Tom Jeffries, your son?"

"Yes."

"Well, what do you know?" He leaned in, a conspiratorial gleam in his eyes. "Do you like surprises, Mrs. Jeffries?"

"I do."

"That's good. But I don't. Would you mind reading me that letter from your son?"

Even the cook shack's fragrant decorations of pine and spruce and the pretty paper chains the children had made couldn't lift Jo's mood. Tom had been so moody since they'd returned from St. Ignace and he'd convinced Frenchie to take him into town a couple times, after which he was more sullen than she'd ever seen him.

Ruth came alongside her at the table and rubbed Jo's shoulders. "Don't give up."

Jo chopped walnuts, cherries, dates, and raisins into the tiniest pieces she could manage. She'd sifted and resifted and then some more trying to get the flour as light as possible. And the hens had obliged by laying just the right sized eggs.

"I haven't given up—I'm just discouraged." She really wanted to make Mrs. Jeffries' fruitcake for Tom.

Mrs. Peyton uncapped the last bottle of vanilla. "We need a miracle, Jo."

The entrance doors to the cook shack swung in.

"It's your Pa and a lady I've never seen before," Mrs. Peyton whispered.

Jo pushed her chair back from the kitchen worktable and stood. The attractive woman, with wavy chestnut hair, was about Jo's height and build and dressed in a heavy wool traveling suit.

Pa held a note card aloft. "Here it is, Jo—straight from your Aunt Hannah's hands."

She sucked in a breath then clapped her hands together. "Do you think it's going to be close enough?"

Pa arched his eyebrows. "After you carrying on and tearing up the house looking for your Ma's recipe, this better be close enough to Mrs. Jeffries' recipe."

The woman's lips twitched. She and Pa exchanged a long glance.

"This is Cordelia, by the way. And she'll be visiting with us. I put her in the Thompson's cottage and the boys are getting a good fire going for her."

"*Cordelia Jeffries?*" Jo's eyes filled with tears as the woman nodded. Jo sped to her and hugged her close as she began to sob. "I …I thought …"

"I'm so sorry, dear. Your father told me you thought I might be dying. But I am fit as Tom's fiddle better be—for I intend to do some dancing tonight."

Jo sniffed, drawing in the scent of lavender and roses. She pulled back and Mrs. Jeffries dabbed Jo's tears with her linen handkerchief. "Now, I think I have some explaining to do. But first, I'd love ever so much to assist you in your baking tonight, Miss Christy."

"But ma'am, your fine clothes will get dirty."

The woman pointed to the wall, where the aprons hung. "Give me the biggest one and I'll keep covered up."

She pulled off her long wool overcoat and Pa hung it on a peg on the wall. Then he assisted Mrs. Jeffries in removing her close fitted jacket. Jo smiled to see Cordelia wore a men's tie over her immaculate white shirt.

"First off, do you have cardamom?"

Jo pulled it from the drawer, where she'd hidden it, saving it for her last effort.

"Thank you, and do you have enough butter, eggs, cream, and flour to make pound cake?"

Pearl offered her hand to Mrs. Jeffries. "I'm Pearl and your son is a right smart young man."

"Thank you. I'm Cordelia and I'm very proud of what a hard worker he is."

"Musta been a long trip up here." Irma pulled the large mixing bowls out from beneath the cupboards.

"Oh, it was, but I wanted to surprise Tom. And I didn't want him to try to talk me out of my plans."

Ruth, covered by a new frilly blue apron from Sven, offered her hand. "I'm Ruth and if it wasn't for your son, I'm not sure I'd be getting married this winter."

"My son, the matchmaker—never thought I'd see the day, not with his history."

"I'll be married soon, too, because of Tom." Pearl grinned at Frenchie, who helped peel potatoes.

"Maybe it's a good thing I wanted to start a business closer to my only son."

"We thought you was sick, Mrs. Jeffries—that is, Cordelia." Irma placed whisks and their handheld beaters beside the bowls.

Tom's mother laughed. "I'm sorry I worried all of you." She sighed. "My comments in the letters were euphemisms."

When all the cooks stared at her, Mrs. Jeffries continued. "It was just a funny way of saying I wasn't going to be on *Ohio* soil much longer—I was taking the train north."

"We're glad you're okay, Cordelia." Pearl patted her arm and then pulled out one of the flour sacks.

"So is your special secret recipe a pound cake?"

"It's a tradition handed down in the Jeffries family for generations. We soak dried fruit in apple cider and add that to the pound cake."

"What a blessing that *you* can make it for him, ma'am." Jo meant every word. The relief she felt at the woman not being sick overcame any last reservations she had about trying to prove to Tom that she could please him. That wasn't what mattered to him. He wanted to make her happy. *Her. The best gift ever.*

"Oh no, you misunderstand. I'll be happy to supervise but I'm not making the fruitcake—you are, Josephine."

Christmas Eve dinner and, with all the families joining them, Tom almost couldn't find a spot to sit. The ladies had outdone themselves with a Northwoods-style feast, after which he'd provide fiddle music and the children would sing the carols they'd practice. What would Jo say when he told her he'd landed a position as a teacher in Mackinaw City? That if they were very careful, and cultivated a large garden, and he hunted, they could manage?

When he'd spied the rows of sliced fruitcake, his mouth had watered. This attempt of Jo's looked exactly how his mother's always did. Maybe it would taste like hers, too. Wouldn't that be something? Regardless, he planned to tell Mr. Christy that if Jo would have him, he wished to marry her after the log drive. Mother had promised she'd get his grandmother's ring to him for the occasion, but it hadn't arrived yet in town. He had, however, received her letter reassuring him that she was fine.

Jo swept toward him, attired in her new red and green gingham dress, looking like a Christmas angel. As she and the other cooks carried trays of fruitcake slices around, Tom tried to catch her attention.

"Jo!"

When she drew near, he reached for a piece, but she slapped his hand. "You have to wait for yours, Mr. Jeffries."

Then she handed all the other men at the table some cake, all except him.

The men laughed. Her brothers rose. From the very back of the room, almost hidden behind all the shanty boys, Mr. Christy stood and a woman seated next to him also rose.

Mother. What on earth was she doing at this camp?

His boss squared his shoulders. "Men, you may recall that Tom told Jo he'd marry her if she baked a fruitcake as good as his mother's."

Tom ducked his head as the men banged their tin mugs on the tables.

"Well, I'm privileged to have a second judge here, tonight, to tell us if the fruitcake Jo has made for this Christmas Eve feast is as good as Tom's mother's. This here is Cordelia Jeffries, who sure oughta know."

Men let out shrill whistles, some clapped, and others hollered their appreciation—as though Mr. Christy had pulled off this feat.

Grinning, Jo came to Tom and tugged at his hand. He wanted to kiss her and kneel down on one knee and propose right then and there. But he could see that everyone was having too much fun with his contest. He tried to make a face as though he was irked but then he burst into laughter.

Pearl placed a chair between the tables and Jo pointed to it. "Sit."

Mr. Christy and Tom's mother stood in front of him. Tom held out his hand to her and she squeezed it. "You found yourself a lovely young lady, son."

Ruth held out a piece of cake on a tin plate, offered as though it were on the finest porcelain dish. His mother released his hand and he took what would be the final dessert challenge.

Mrs. Peyton handed him a fork. "Eat up, Tom. The whole camp is waiting."

He took a bite and closed his eyes. Memories of Christmas traditions at home ran through his mind. Father reading from Luke's account of Christ's birth. Emily and him checking the gifts they'd made for their parents and trying to sneak a peek at the Christmas tree before the parlor doors were opened. Mother finishing up the mittens she knitted them every year. Grandfather driving up in his carriage and later pronouncing Mother's fruitcake "the best ever."

The noise in the room dissipated. This was real. He was about to propose.

Mr. Christy cleared his throat. "Thought I better mention to Tom that we have a tradition in our family, too."

Jo frowned. "What's that, Pa?"

He reached into his chest pocket and drew out a large envelope. "A gift for a child going out on their own."

"She won't be on her own, sir." Tom stood. "This fruitcake tastes just like my mother's!" He swept his mother into his arms and twirled her around.

Mr. Christy tapped him on his shoulder. "But your new wife would be running a bakery."

Coming alongside Tom, Jo squeezed his arm. He leaned over to kiss her cheek and the men hooted and hollered again.

"Pa, the bakery in St. Ignace is out of business." Jo cocked her head at her father as he shoved the envelope at her.

"This one is in Mackinaw City."

"What?" She opened the letter.

Tom peered over her shoulder. The paperwork inside appeared to be legal title to the old bakery on Nicolet Street.

His mother took the papers from Jo. "Why that's right near my new restaurant. We'll have to talk business later, Josephine."

Pa hauled her up into a bear hug. "That's from your Ma and me—we'd been puttin' a little aside for a long time for you and I know she'd want you to have this now."

All around them, everyone chipped in to clean up from the feast. Tom still held her hand tight, as though she might run off.

"Thank you." Jo kissed her father's stubbly cheek.

"My ma, your grandma Christy, gave each of us property to get us started, the Christmas we were old enough to be married. Your ma and I wanted the same for you."

Jo was humbled by her parents' gift. They'd scrimped and done without so that she could be independent, if she so chose. What a sacrifice they'd made.

"I met with the lawyer who comes to town and everything is all legal. Also put some money in the bank, so you can buy what you need to get started."

"I don't know what to say."

"Your happiness is sweeter than any words you have for me." Pa squeezed her hand then turned to face Tom.

"Sir, I do need to speak with you. I intend to marry Jo and I've been hired to teach here in town, next year."

"Good."

"Good?" Hadn't he wanted him to work at the new camp?

"Shows some gumption on your part. And I think you'll be better suited to town life with Jo."

Tom didn't know what to say.

"If you'll excuse me," Mr. Christy boomed, "I'd like to have another piece of cake and some coffee before it's all gone." With that, the camp boss lumbered off toward the kitchen.

Mother smiled up at him. "Congratulations, son. I'm so happy for you and Jo."

"Thank you for the recipe, Mrs. Jeffries."

"You are very welcome. But if I know my son, he was already planning to propose." She pulled a battered wood box from her pocket and handed it to him.

"Sit down, Jo." Tom guided her to the chair and she obliged.

He opened the box, bent down on one knee and took her left hand in his. "Would you do me the honor of becoming my wife?"

Her eyes filled with tears. "Yes," she whispered.

He removed the ring, centered with a round sapphire as blue as the straits of Mackinac, encircled by small diamonds. Jo gasped as he slid it onto her ring finger.

Pearl, Irma, Mrs. Peyton, Ox and Moose, Mr. Brevort, Ruth and Sven, all surrounded them. The click of nails on the wood floor announced Blue Dog as he nudged his way closer and rubbed his nose against Tom's knee.

Jo patted Blue Dog's head. "You weren't going to miss out on this, were you?"

Laughing, Tom closed the jewelry box and tucked it into his pocket.

His mother patted his shoulder. "You've got what looks a cloud of witnesses."

He wouldn't have it any other way. He'd come to love these people, who meant the world to Jo. He'd ensure they saw them often.

Jo stared down at the beautiful ring on her finger. Engaged. Owning a shop. Having his mother help her like a ministering angel. This was a Christmas she'd never forget. And to think, only a few days earlier, she'd had no hope.

But God had other plans. Plans that included Tom. Plans giving her a hope *and* a future.

The End

Author's Notes

Michigan's white pines were massive; virgin forest, which was cut and sold off for so much profit that it was referred to as "White Gold." These trees built much of the housing boom around the Great Lakes, such as in Chicago, during the mid to late 1800's. When an area was logged off, a new camp had to be set up. Consequently, many of the lumberjack bosses were heading further North, eventually to the Upper Peninsula. My grandfather ran "Skidmore Camp" in Newberry, in the central U.P. By the 1890's, lumberjacks were beginning to find the lower peninsula logged out of white pine. The U.P. also boasts fine hardwoods—another draw.

Camp life was difficult. Others authors have written about more of the tragedies and hard life people suffered in the lumber industry. This is a Christmas novella about hope, so you won't find too much dwelling on hardships. However, I do include one villain, inspired by research and by real events (the latter being modern day, however.) Most camps were composed completely of men but there were some "family camps" and my grandfather ran one later, in the 1940's and 1950's. Although from Kentucky, my grandpa Christy Skidmore was born in Traverse City. I'm surmising that my great-grandmother, Rebecca "Bessie" Christy Skidmore Sexton, was with my great-grandfather while he was up North lumbering. They resided in Kentucky.

As can be imagined, women in turn-of-the-century Michigan and elsewhere were fighting a battle for more independence. And women were finally able to pursue higher education, albeit in limited locations. Jo wants her right to choose where she's going to live and what she's going to do. She despises feeling "stuck" as many women did.

Schoolteachers during this time frame were primarily taught in what were called "Normal Schools" and my hero, Tom attended one of these in Ohio, a state known for its public education movement. Teachers during the late 1800's lived under a ridiculous set of rules and expectations. They were paid very little for their hard work.

If you get a chance to visit, Newberry's Tahquamenon Logging Museum has an amazing assortment of lumbering artifacts. Don't miss out on a trip to Hartwick Pines in the lower peninsula of Michigan. The beauty of the forest will take you back to a time long ago—like I hope this story did!

Thank you for reading The Fruitcake Challenge, a Selah Award finalist. If you'd like to connect with me, visit my website at www.carriefancettpagels.com. If you'd like to sign up for my newsletter, check under the "Contact" page. And look under the "Books" page for my other publications, including

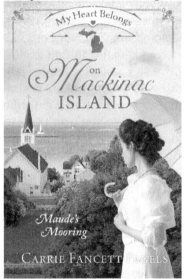

Maggie Award winner, "My Heart Belongs on Mackinac Island"

Holt Medallion finalist, *The Steeplechase*

Maggie Awards finalist, *The Substitute Bride*

And more!

Made in the USA
Middletown, DE
06 February 2022